TRAPPED!

As Shorty approached one of the windows, a shot blasted close by and he ducked away, seeing flashes of light suddenly. He had almost looked into the muzzle of a gun.

He retreated, momentarily blinded. More shots searched for him as he dropped to the floor. They smashed into the walls and one hit a lantern, shattering it to bits. Shorty crawled into the next room, breathing hard.

There were at least two of them!

This was a tight spot! He blinked, letting his eyes come back to normal. What the hell was he going to do?

Then he smelled smoke. . . .

THE STEEL BOX

Arthur Moore

FAWCETT GOLD MEDAL • NEW YORK

A Fawcett Gold Medal Book
Published by Ballantine Books
Copyright © 1989 by Arthur Moore

Library of Congress Catalog Card Number: 88-92928

ISBN 0-449-14549-2

Manufactured in the United States of America

First Edition: June 1989

Chapter One

WHEN Laredo and Pete Torres arrived at the Treasury Building, Fleming was pacing the steps, smoking furiously. John R. Fleming was Chief of Security Operations, West. He was a large, paunchy man whose clothes were dusted with ashes. He was almost never seen without a cigar. His sleeves had burn holes, and his subordinates swore they could smell him a block away.

Fleming acknowledged their presence with a nod and a brief, "Thanks for hurrying."

"Emergency?" Laredo asked.

"It's that goddam Quinlan again," Fleming said in a growling voice. "The man's got the brains of a chipmunk. It's a disgrace they keep him on."

"Who's Quinlan?" Pete asked.

Fleming made a rude gesture. "His name's Gerard Quinlan. He's a Treasury agent—God knows how. The sonofabitch must know where a body's buried." He waved the cigar at them. "I want you two on the way to Nevada tonight. Can you do it?"

"Nevada!" Pete said.

"Where in Nevada?"

"Carson City." Fleming glanced around casually; there was no one near them. It was a brisk day, cold even at noon, and people were bundled up against the chill wind.

Fleming went on. "The department has scraped together a shipment consisting of several million dollars in bills, gold coin, and gems, and they would like to see it brought back here to Washington without every goddam crook in the country grabbing a share of it."

"So it's hush-hush top secret," Pete said.

"You damn betcha. So far only a couple of people know about it." Fleming pointed to them. "I just added two more."

Laredo smiled. He was a tawny-haired young man with regular, rather square features. The gray suit coat he wore seemed somehow too small for his shoulders. He rubbed his jaw. "And this Gerard Quinlan you mentioned is in charge of it?"

"Unfortunately, yes. He's been assigned to bring it here. Of course, he will mess it up and probably lose it on the way."

"You have faith in him."

"Every faith that he will stumble over his own feet. But the powers that be think he is just the man for the job." Fleming shrugged and puffed the cigar. "They are stupid, of course." Fleming usually spoke his mind. "And I told them so—not in those words. But I stuck my neck out."

"In what way?"

"I assured them that Quinlan would fail, and that I'd have to send you in."

"But he hasn't failed *yet*?"

Fleming puffed and looked at the glowing end of the cigar. "He may have. I don't know. But I'm sending you out there just the same. I know Quinlan. If it is possible to muck it up, he will do it. And unfortunately, if he does, the government will have lost millions in seizures. And in a way it will reflect on me—even though I had no part in selecting the fool."

2

Laredo glanced at Pete. "So our official position is like always?"

"Yes. What hotel are you staying at?"

"The Hampshire."

"All right. I'll have your credentials sent there within hours. As usual, you'll have full authority from this office, and your job is to see that the shipment comes here to me in Washington."

Pete grinned. "No questions asked?"

"I don't care what the hell you have to do to get it here. And if Quinlan gets in the way, kiok his ass, and one for me." He looked at both of them. "Is that clear enough?"

"I like the clarity," Pete said, grinning. He was a big man, slightly larger in bulk than Laredo. He was dark, with hair the color of coal dipped in water; his eyes were ebon and he was a top-of-the-class graduate of the Tanner Training Center near Springfield, as was Laredo. They had met at the school and been posted first and second in the class, most of which had failed and been sent home. The Tanner Detective Organization did work almost exclusively for the government.

Fleming was dependable. The credentials arrived by special messenger in two hours, along with money and names. They were directed to report to Doyle Reinhardt, the Treasury Department man in Carson City. Reinhardt would brief them about the situation, Quinlan, and the shipment.

A note from Fleming said that Reinhardt was to be trusted. "He is a personal friend and thinks the same as I do about Quinlan."

Laredo talked to the desk clerk, who had a sheaf of train schedules. "There's a rattler leaving for Chicago at ten to-night," the clerk said. "You want me to get the tickets?"

"Please," Laredo agreed.

He went back upstairs and packed a bag. Pete was already set to go. At nine-fifteen they went down and hailed a cab and were driven to the railroad station.

* * *

The Secretary of the Treasury had long since sent round a personal order to all department heads concerning secrecy. "This department," he wrote, "is inevitably involved in many areas that must remain secret, or there will be failures."

It was a need-to-know order and was strictly enforced —when that was possible.

Victor Kolby was a slim, slightly pot-bellied, middle-aged man with sparse hair and steel-rimmed glasses. He was temporarily in charge of his department at the Treasury, while his superior was absent with a bad attack of food poisoning that kept him in bed. A great many papers crossed Kolby's desk daily, some requiring his initials or signature.

Then one morning an envelope was hand-delivered, stamped SECRET. The messenger had a pad, and Kolby signed for the thin envelope and got a receipt. This was the first such he'd signed for. It was all glued together with heavy paper, addressed to the head of the department.

Kolby stared at it, gripping his lower lip with his teeth. What the hell was in it? This kind of thing happened once in a while, he knew, and each time he'd seen such an envelope on his boss's desk he had been fascinated.

He put it aside, but his thoughts kept coming back to it. He was aware, as was everyone, that secret information frequently came to high government officials which, if acted upon, could make the official wealthy. Of course if one took that route it would be necessary to be enormously circumspect—to deal through third or fourth parties—but it could be done. Office gossip said it had been done.

Was there information of that sort in the envelope?

He handled it when no one was near, picking at the glue. How would he know what was inside unless he opened it? But it did not bear his name. The rules said he must hand it over to the department head.

It was brown and not at all thick. Apparently there were only a couple sheets of paper inside. But it *had* to be important, or else it would never be marked SECRET.

God! What a temptation! Maybe wealth was at his fingertips. If only he had the guts to do something about it.

Kolby often took ordinary papers home with him, to deal with in the evenings. If he had spent too much time gossiping in the office, it was necessary to do so. That night he took the secret envelope as well. Somewhere he had heard that one could steam open such an envelope. Maybe he should try it.

He lived alone in a two-room flat within walking distance of the office. It was his habit to fix himself soup or other food over a gas jet. The practice was frowned on but he did it anyway. He heated some leftover pork and ate it with a slice of bread, the brown envelope propped up on the table before him.

If staring at it would cause the glue to fail, the flap would have popped open long since.

Of course if he opened the envelope and it tore, or the flap could not be put back—then what? He dared not destroy it. He could not claim he'd never received it—they had his signature. If he said it had been stolen it would go on his record and promotion would pass him by for sure ... after he faced the police questions. And he certainly could not admit he'd taken it home. That was against the rules too.

Kolby swore, looking at it. What the hell was inside?

Finally he filled a kettle and put it over the gas jet. When steam was spouting from the neck he held the envelope in its path very carefully, moving it back and forth till the glue softened. And it did soften!

To his delight, the flap came open! He took the paper out. It was a memo to certain department heads, informing them that a shipment of specie, gems, and documents was expected to reach Washington in the very near future from Carson City, Nevada. The value was presumed to be in excess of two million dollars and each department head was referred to Special Order C-154/63 and would be called upon for the Action Report expected as per the meeting 27 August last.

Kolby's heart pounded, and the paper shook in his hand. In excess of two million dollars! He could hardly comprehend such a fortune. He had to wait, to calm himself down, before he could slip the paper back into the envelope. He could not trust himself to re-seal it but put it aside for later. In excess of two million dollars!

A vast spill of gold coins seemed to infest his brain, a shimmering, clinking pile—God! What could he do with that much money? What could he *not* do! It made him dizzy to think about it.

He blew out his breath and forced himself to shake off all that and think calmly. What he had was really only *information*. A shipment was about to leave Carson City for Washington. And probably well guarded.

What could he do with that information? Nothing at all by himself. He wouldn't know how to go about taking it from trained guards.

He would have to sell it. Sell the information. He would have to sell the information to someone for a percentage or outright. He sighed deeply. If he sold it, the buyer would have to be a crook. It was against the law to steal, especially millions of dollars. And the chances that a crook would give him a percentage of the take was unlikely. The crook would take it all. No, he would have to sell it outright.

But who would he sell it to?

He did not know any crooks and could not advertise for one. How did you reach a crook? He had heard of the underworld, but had no idea where it was.

Wait a minute—what about Pinto Yoder?

Pinto was a small-timer who had thought himself a confidence man. Kolby had met him once through a restaurant owner in Washington. Pinto was the owner's nephew, a man who had gotten himself involved with a Treasury agent who had him cold and was talking jail.

All this had happened three years ago. Kolby had arranged a meeting between the agent and the restaurant

6

owner and they had worked it all out with the payment of certain monies—but no jail.

The restaurant owner had been grateful to Kolby and had written off all Kolby's chits. He had had free meals for a period of four months.

Pinto had said he was grateful too.

Kolby spent the most restless night of his life. But in the morning he felt calm and was able to re-seal the envelope so it looked perfectly normal.

At the office he chatted with a dozen men and by nightfall had listened to some very interesting information. It was astonishing how men prattled to others in the same line of work.

He learned that Doyle Reinhardt, recently posted from the South, was now the top Treasury man in Carson City, capital of Nevada. He also heard that Gerard Quinlan was in charge of something or other, very hush-hush, in that far city.

And almost by chance he heard that the famous Tanner Organization was being employed by Fleming's section. Several men were being sent west. No one knew very much about this, so it was largely speculation.

No one mentioned the shipment, but Kolby had no doubts about why Carson City was so attractive all of a sudden. The town was a dot on the map, a two-bit dot at that. So all the action centering about it was very unusual.

Several millions unusual.

On Saturday next he went to look up Pinto Yoder.

Chapter Two

PINTO was glad to see Victor Kolby, and not a little surprised as well. Pinto was a small man, wizened before his years, and very shifty-eyed, a thing he apparently could not control. This last was unfortunate, a habit picked up in jail. Unfortunate because it curtailed his interests, making prospective confidence victims sheer off. A man attempting to sell blue-sky mining stock, for instance, should have a steady, impressive gaze, exuding honesty.

So, because of this failing, Pinto worked in a shoe factory part-time. His uncle, the restaurant owner, gave Kolby the address of Pinto's boardinghouse and Pinto shook his hand when Kolby came round one evening.

"Well—it's Mr. Kolby! Come in, come in. . . ." Pinto's face showed his curiosity. He had never expected to see Kolby again. "Wot can I do f'you?"

Kolby shut the door and sat, glancing about him. He was in a cheap little one-room lodging that contained heavy, badly made and painted furniture without cushions. The room smelled worse than a fish market. Obviously Pinto no longer noticed.

Victor had thought how to begin; he knew Pinto would be surprised at his coming. "I need your help, Pinto. I'm willing to pay a bit—not too much. I don't have much, you understand." This said with a smile to take any sting out.

"Help? How c'n I help the likes of you, Mr. Kolby?"

"I need someone who can finance a deal. It'll take a lot of money."

Pinto nodded, looking at his visitor sidelong. Kolby was an odd duck, he thought. And if he had come to Pinto Yoder, didn't it mean that this deal he mentioned was shady? Otherwise wouldn't he go to a bank?

Pinto nodded again. "I see." But he didn't see. "Wot kind of a deal?"

"It's very complicated," Kolby said. "It'll require a lot of traveling and maybe some fighting."

"Fighting!" Pinto made a face. "But there's a payoff?"

Kolby smiled. "A good fat payoff." He leaned forward. "Do you know someone who can finance it? If you do there'll be a cut in it for both of us."'

"A cut if the thing is pulled off, you mean."

"Yes, of course."

Pinto grinned. "You know something, huh Mr. Kolby? Is that it?"'

"That's right. I know something. I can't do this myself. I'm not a fighting man for one thing."

"There's a danger, huh?"

"I think so, yes. But it's worth it."

Pinto got up and wandered about the room, turning it over in his mind. Someone with the money to finance a deal? . . . He sighed inwardly. Fritz Benner was obviously the man. But Benner was mean as a teased snake and could be trusted possibly halfway across the room. Benner would promise the moon and deliver moonbeams.

But he did have the money to finance any deal that Kolby was likely to come up with. And Pinto could think of no one else who did. His uncle might have, but he'd never enter into a shady operation; he had no guts.

9

The big trouble with Benner was that he would undoubtedly wind up with all the loot or merchandise or whatever Kolby had. Benner was tight and ruthless. But of course all that was Kolby's problem. He would steer the two together and hope that something would drop into his, Pinto's, lap.

"Fritz Benner," he said. "But I got to tell you, he's greedy as a politician."

"He has the money?"

"Oh yes." Pinto nodded vigorously. "But don't depend on him for shares."

"I see. A grasping sort . . ."

Pinto nodded.

"Can you put me together with this Mr. Benner?" Kolby cleared his throat. "Not in broad daylight."

Pinto smiled. Now he *knew* it was shady. "Yes, but gimme a day'r so. Me and Benner, we don't travel in the same social circles, you know."

Kolby had a card ready and handed it over. "This's where I live." He got up to go. "Keep it to yourself—I mean about seeing me."

"Of course, of course." Pinto smiled. "Allus a pleasure, Mr. Kolby." He waved the card. "I'll come as soon's I talk to Benner."

"Fine."

Fritz Benner would consider him no better than a doormat, Pinto knew. Benner would probably not see him without plenty of reason and cause. Pinto left word in several saloons where he thought Benner was well known that he had something that would interest Mr. Benner.

And he was astonished when Benner showed up at his smelly flat, pushing his way in, then holding his nose, glaring at the frightened Pinto. "What the hell is dead in here?"

It was not a question that demanded an answer. Pinto winced and pointed to chairs. Benner had someone with him who stayed outside the door. Benner pulled a chair

10

around to face Pinto, his face a mask of disgust. "Out with it. What you got, Pinto?"

"I got—something to sell. I mean I know somebody who wants to sell you something."

"Yeh? What is it?"

"Information."

"All right. Information about what?"

"He has to tell you."

"Then what the hell am I doing here?"

Pinto cringed. "I dunno what it is—he wouldn't tell me. All's I know is it's a deal that needs money to work it."

"Who is this man?"

"He works for the gov'ment."

"Ahhhh." Benner's manner changed subtly. "A government man—with information to sell." He stared at Pinto, making the little man exceedingly nervous. "Tell me, how well do you know this man?"

Pinto shrugged thin shoulders. "Not too well."

"How'd he come to you then?"

"My uncle. He knows 'im."

"I see." Benner frowned at the other for a moment, then made up his mind. "All right. Tell him to be at the east gate of Goode Park at midday tomorrow with a piece of yellow paper in his hand so I'll know him. You got that?"

Pinto nodded. "He wants to meet you at night."

"He'll do what I tell him." Benner rose. "I'll pick him up in my carriage." He went out without another word.

Pinto went to Kolby's door and waited nearby till the bureaucrat came out on his way to work in the morning. He quickly related what Benner had said. "He'll talk to you."

"Good. I'll be there."

"And remember my cut."

"Of course."

Victor was at the Goode Street gate promptly, several minutes early in fact. In the office he had torn a piece of

11

yellow cardboard to a small, pocket-sized square, and now held it in his hand, peering closely at every carriage that approached.

Ten minutes after noon a black and tan carriage drew up, and an arm beckoned to him. Kolby ran and climbed in, dropping the cardboard. The door slammed, and he was seated beside a bulky man dressed in an expensive, fur-collared overcoat and beaver hat. A diamond stickpin glittered under his fleshy chin.

The man eyed him, turning his head slightly. "I'm Benner." He did not offer to shake hands.

"Victor Kolby."

"You work for the government, I'm told." The carriage moved on, creaking and clattering over the rutted street behind the clip-clopping horse.

"Yes. In the Treasury Department." Benner looked like a senator, Kolby thought. The man's voice was modulated and rather cold, and so were his eyes. Kolby had the feeling that Benner was not a man to cross.

"And you have information to sell?"

Kolby hesitated. Benner turned his head and stared at him, and Kolby nodded. This was the point of no return. He had to deal or get out of the carriage.

Benner said, "What you tell me will go no farther." He indicated the driver on the box. "He cannot hear us. Your name will never be mentioned by me."

"I—I could be ruined," Kolby said, taking a breath.

"Yes. I assure you I deal with men in government all the time, many times in complete secrecy. You will be no exception. Now—what is the information?"

"I—I know about a shipment that contains items worth several millions."

"The property of the government?"

"Yes."

Benner was silent for a moment and Kolby looked out to see that they were slowly circling the park. He looked at Benner and saw that he was gently tapping a finger against his lips.

Kolby shifted uncomfortably, and Benner said, "And what sort of an arrangement were you contemplating?"

"I thought I might—sell the information."

"Yes, so you said."

Kolby cleared his throat nervously. "The shipment is worth a couple million—maybe more if it's sold carefully. I ought to get five percent."

Benner looked at him again. "Five percent of two million dollars is one hundred thousand." He shook his head. "A very tidy amount."

"But a trifle beside two million!"

"Perhaps. Perhaps. But it's too much. If your information is good I'll give you a thousand."

"One thousand dollars!" Kolby was astonished.

"My dear Kolby, I am taking all the risks. Can you guarantee that this rich morsel will fall into my hands without a fight or trouble of any kind? No? I thought not. In fact I may even be out the thousand I pay you. You are giving me only information, not a shred of help."

"But—but—"

"Where is this package? Here in the city?"

"No," said Kolby in a small voice. "A long way off."

"A long way off," echoed Benner, staring at him. "Worse still! It will cost me wages for men to go after it—perhaps train fare and food money—hotels—the bills run up!" He shook his head sadly. "It sounds less and less interesting when you begin to add up the totals."

"But it's two million dollars' worth!"

"It might cost me two million to get it," Benner said gruffly. "And trouble with the law to boot."

Kolby stared at the floor. All his dreams were fading fast. Maybe he should never have opened that damned envelope.

"I will drive you back to the gate," Benner said. "I'm sorry, Mr. Kolby, but a thousand is my best offer. And I assure you I'm having second thoughts about that."

So was Kolby. The obstacles, as presented by Benner, seemed enormous.

13

Kolby looked ahead, seeing the gate approach. He said dully, "All right, Mr. Benner, a thousand."

The other nodded. "Now the details, please."

Kolby told him about the shipment that would go out from Carson City. He mentioned Doyle Reinhardt and Gerard Quinlan, saying that many thought Quinlan an ass and inept. "But he is in charge and will probably have two or three men under him. They are expected to take the train."

Benner made notes. "Is that it?"

Kolby did not mention the Tanner Organization. If he was only being paid a thousand, let Benner find out about that himself.

"How will this shipment be packaged?"

"Probably in a steel box, marked U.S. Government, Treasury Department." Kolby held his hands out about eighteen inches apart. "The boxes are about this square, unpainted metal with a lock. I expect Quinlan will have the key."

"What does Quinlan look like?"

"I've never seen him. They'll put the box in the baggage compartment of the train. You'll find him there."

Benner stopped the carriage at the gate. Reaching into an inner pocket, he drew out a wad of greenbacks. He counted out one thousand dollars and handed it over. "I warn you, say nothing of this to anyone . . . not anyone!"

"Of course not!" Kolby put the money away. He nodded and climbed out, slamming the door. The driver slapped the reins at once, and Kolby watched the carriage clatter away. Had he been snookered? He felt as if he had. Benner was a smooth sonofabitch! He felt the bulk of the bills and sighed. Still, a thousand dollars for doing nothing but riding in a carriage wasn't bad. He would never get rich that way, but . . .

He turned and walked through the park. Under a clump of trees, he glanced around and took out the money and divided it, putting half in a hip pocket.

When he met Pinto later, he told the little man about his

ride around the park with Benner. "He didn't think much of the deal."

Pinto was surprised. "He didn't buy it?"

"Well, he gave me a dozen reasons why it probably wouldn't work."

"Damn him!"

"But he gave me five hundred," Kolby lied.

Pinto brightened. "Well, that's better'n nothing, hey?"

He watched Kolby take out the bills. Kolby handed over fifty dollars.

"Benner got two million and he gave me nothing. When you deal with crooks— Oh, pardon me, Pinto, no offense."

Pinto sighed. "Course not." He fingered the bills and put them in his pocket. He should have gotten a hundred. When you deal with politicians . . .

15

Chapter Three

NEITHER Laredo nor Pete liked riding long distances in trains, so the journey to Chicago was tiresome in the extreme. It was necessary to change trains twice, and there was an unexpected layover in Ohio because of a collapsed trestle bridge.

However, Laredo was philosophical and curled up to get as much sleep as possible. He could do nothing about the train or the track problems so he would ignore them. Of course there would come times when sleep would be impossible, so, he told Pete, "Enjoy it while you can."

Could a man store up sleep to use later when needed?

It was a foolish idea, Pete said, but then Pete was very practical. "That's like saying that if you drink a gallon of water today you won't be thirsty for a week."

Laredo yawned. "Who could drink a gallon of water at one sitting?"

"It's just an example."

Laredo turned over. "Wake me for supper, huh?"

* * *

The weather was not the best when they reached Chicago—which was now being called the Gem of the Prairie. It was overly hot and humid; the winds off the lake seemed heated instead of cool. But they were glad to leave the dusty train behind—for the time being.

The conductor had told them they must change trains if they were going farther west. When Laredo asked why the same train could not take them on, the conductor said the Big Brass had decided everyone changed trains. That was the way it was. Probably it put money in someone's pockets to do it that way.

There were any number of small hotels and boarding-houses in the city, many within walking distance of the train depot. It would be necessary for them to stay overnight and take the train west in the morning. Apparently no one coordinated these things.

They walked from the station carrying their baggage and found a smallish, clean-looking hotel in the third block, the Hamilton. The clerk on duty was a student, a friendly young man working his way through college, he told them. Yes, he had a dozen rooms; this was a quiet time of year.

"You can have almost any room in the house."

They signed for two small rooms on the second floor. The bathroom was just down the hall. There was plenty of hot water.

"Exactly what I want," Pete said, "lots of water in a tub."

There was also a restaurant at the end of the block, the clerk told them. "It stays open"—he glanced at the lobby clock—"for about two more hours."

"Thanks," Laredo said. "Can we bring you back something?"

"I've got a lunch pail with me." The young man smiled. "I eat at midnight. But thanks for the offer."

It proved to be a good restaurant, mostly empty at that hour. They depended on train passenger traffic, a waiter said. There would be a nice crowd before midnight when the eastbound got in.

17

They ate beef and red beans, with apple pie and coffee to round it out. The food on the train had been minimal or nothing. They'd had to depend on running to a café at the train stops, and running back in time to swing aboard. Not much of a system; it desperately needed improvement.

Pete rolled a cigarette to smoke with his coffee, then they strolled back to the hotel as people began to stream from the depot. There were several hundred, some getting into cabs, others passing in carriages—probably those lucky enough to be picked up.

A dozen people were in the lobby, surrounded by piles of luggage. A second clerk was on duty. When he noticed Pete and Laredo, the young man who had registered them came out from behind the counter with a folded piece of paper saying loudly, "Sirs—here's the brochure you requested."

He gave the folder to Laredo, who thanked him gravely. They had requested nothing; he thought the look on the clerk's face was curious. The clerk hurried back around the desk immediately and plunged into assigning rooms.

Laredo and Pete went up the steps quickly and into Laredo's room. Pete said, "What brochure is that?"

Laredo lighted the gas jet and opened the folder. A note fell out. Pete picked it up and read:

> This man was asking for you. I
> remember you saying you knew no one
> in Chicago, so I thought it was
> peculiar. If it means nothing,
> then tear this up.

It was signed "Harry." And there was a pencil drawing of a half-bearded man with mean eyes and a wide, flat mouth.

"Harry must be an art student," Pete remarked. "It's pretty good. D'you know him?"

Laredo shook his head. "Well, Harry is a friend of ours all right. This sketch is as good as a tintype." Laredo stud-

18

ied it. He had never seen the man before but he would probably know him instantly. Pete thought the same.

Pete propped the sketch up on the round table. "No one knew we'd be in this hotel. We didn't know ourselves. We picked it at random. That means—"

"Someone followed us from the station."

"Yes. And Harry saw one of them, but there may be more." Pete grinned. "Do you suppose somebody wants to keep us from going to Carson City?"

"Well, somebody knows about the shipment. That's for sure."

Pete slipped his Colt revolver from a shoulder holster, pulled the hammer to half-cock, and spun the cylinder by rolling it down his arm. He looked at the bright primer ends; the pistol was fully loaded. He put it away.

Laredo said, "As I see it, we have two choices."

"Yes?"

"We can slide out of here tonight and let this *hombre* hold the bag." He pointed at the drawing. "Or we can hang around and see who else is involved."

"And maybe bend them in certain places where they were not designed to bend?"

"We'll play that part of it by ear. What's your vote?"

Pete smiled. "I vote we hang around. I get nervous when people are following me. So you figure we're slated to push up daisies?"

Laredo looked at his partner in surprise. "Of course. Why d'you think they're following us?"

"Then there's definitely more than one. You think they know who we are?"

"I'd guess so." Laredo frowned at the door. It looked solid enough. Pete saw the look and turned.

"They won't come in the door. They'll wait and try for us on the stairs or in the hall. They don't know what they face if they come in the door."

Laredo agreed. "It might be smart for both of us to stay in one room."

They put a chair back under the door handle and it

proved to be an uneventful night. If someone tried the door, they did not detect it.

In the morning they joined other people on the street and walked to the restaurant for breakfast, on the theory that an assassin might hesitate to shoot them when they were surrounded by others. It was apparently a sound theory.

They ate with backs to the wall and saw no one that looked like the drawing.

From the restaurant they went to the telegraph office and composed a coded wire to John Fleming saying that they were being followed in Chicago. Perhaps he could research the Washington, D.C., end to turn up an enemy. Someone who should not know obviously knew about the shipment.

For the benefit of a follower, they next went to the stagecoach office and inquired about routes west. It should cause the follower to become concerned. Would they take the train or the stage? If, of course, they lived to escape the Windy City.

In their walks, Pete thought he had spotted the tail, a fellow in a rusty-looking coat and a bowler hat. He was not positive, but the man seemed to drift along behind them on the opposite side of the street.

When they returned to the hotel, Laredo looked through the front window to the street. The man in the bowler hat stopped across from the hotel front door, pulled out a news-paper, and began to read it. Pete nodded. "That's him."

"Where's the other one?"

"He could be on this side of the street where we can't see him."

Laredo scratched his chin. "We've got two choices again."

"Lose them or fight them?"

"Yes. We've got to lose them before we get on the train, or we'll have to force the action. We can't have them skulking along behind us all the way to Nevada."

"We go out and shoot it out?"

20

Laredo said, "There's a public park a couple of streets over. . . . Maybe they'll follow us there."

"Do we give them a chance to tell us why they're after us and who's paying them?"

Laredo shrugged. "They won't tell us."

"There are ways."

Laredo grinned. "I'll bet there's not an anthill to tie them onto within a thousand miles."

Pete sighed. "I think you're part Apache."

"Let's go to the park."

They strolled out to the street behind a gaggle of elderly ladies. Out of the corner of his eye Laredo saw Bowler Hat put down the newspaper in a hurry.

He must have signaled the other man, because as they turned into a side street Laredo saw the second, the man the night clerk had sketched. He fell in behind them and Laredo mentioned it to Pete.

"Two against two," Pete said. "Better odds than usual."

The park was not large, with clumps of trees and shrubbery turning bright green. There were several paths winding through it, and Laredo could see no other park visitors. It was probably early for women with babies. . . .

They walked to the center of the grassy area and paused. They were separated, a dozen feet apart. Laredo turned, the Colt revolver down at his side, hidden from the followers. Pete did the same.

As they turned the two pursuers halted. No words were spoken at all.

Bowler Hat wore a long coat, and as he halted he pulled a shortened double-barreled shotgun from its skirts. As he lifted it toward them, both Laredo and Pete fired. The shotgun boomed into the sky.

The bearded man fired at them, five shots as fast as he could pull trigger. Then he ran.

Both Pete and Laredo dropped to the ground. Laredo's second shot made the running man swerve and stumble, but he continued. They let him go. He would be on the main street in a moment and it was no good firing into crowds.

Laredo looked at Pete. "You all right?"

"Never touched me."

They got up and walked to Bowler Hat, rolling him over, faceup. His hat had rolled away. He was dead as he would ever be. Pete searched him, finding a letter addressed to William Amend. He had a few bills, some coins, a cigar cutter, and three keys.

"Guess his name is Amend," Pete said.

"It's amen now," Laredo replied. "Let's get out of here."

A small crowd had gathered at the park entrance, drawn by the sounds of gunshots. Laredo put the envelope in his pocket and they left the body behind, walking rapidly toward the main street. People stared at them but no one protested their going.

Pete said, "The train isn't due for hours."

"Not good. If we stay around the police are going to be breathing down our necks. A dozen people saw us. . . ."

"The hotel clerk can sketch us."

Laredo laughed. "We'd best get our possibles and take the stage. What you think?"

"I say yes. And we ought to wire Fleming."

"At the next town."

They checked out of the hotel and hurried to the stage depot, buying tickets for Kansas City.

No policeman stopped them as the stage rolled out and headed west.

Fritz Benner was certain the information Kolby had given him was accurate; Kolby would not dare lie to him. But he paid for corroboration just the same. He had certain contacts who verified much of what Kolby had said, and added something else.

The Tanner Organization had been called in by the Fleming Security Section. Two men, top agents, had been

22

ordered west to Carson City. It cost him a hundred dollars to learn their names.

Immediately Benner wired Erich Ganz in Milwaukee: "Go at once to Chicago." Ganz ran to take the stage, only a short hop. The long night wire contained the names of two men, Laredo Garrett and Pedro Torres, with descriptions of each. These two men were to be totally eliminated; that fact was in code. Ganz, dark-bearded and slight, had worked for Benner many times in the past and was to be paid five hundred dollars for the chore. How he did the job was his to decide. Benner cared only about results.

That was all he had to go on. Damned little. And Chicago was a big city. How would he find two men in it? Benner said the two had gone by train; they were leaving at once, according to Benner's contacts.

So Ganz hired Will Amend, promising him a hundred dollars on the demise of the two victims. Ganz did not tell Will what kind of men he would face. He did not know himself.

The only chance they had was to watch the incoming trains.

This paid off inside of two days. They spotted two men who fit the descriptions exactly, as they stepped off the train from Washington, D.C. And they lost the two immediately in the crowds.

Ganz hurried to the cab ranks and watched each person who took a hack—and did not see the two.

"They're walking to a hotel," he told Amend. "We'll split up and ask at each hotel within a mile or so. Say we're friends and missed them at the station."

Amend nodded and set out.

Ganz found them himself the next day. The two victims had put up at the Hamilton Hotel. He and Will followed them as they went here and there, each tailing on opposite sides of the street. They hoped to find the two at a disadvantage, but no chance came. It was frustrating. It was almost as if they had been spotted. But probably not; it was

23

just chance that the two were usually in a crowd. After all, they were only ordinary citizens. . . .

When the two men walked from the hotel finally, and headed for the little park, Ganz was delighted. Will Amend had his sawed-off shotgun hanging by a string inside his long coat. It alone would make short work of the two pigeons.

But in the park when the two men halted and turned, Will raised the shotgun—and was immediately shot down! Ganz was shocked. He fired wildly, turned, and ran. These men were deadly shots! You sonofabitch, Benner! You didn't tell me enough!

A shot creased his upper arm, but he got away.

Nothing had gone right! He hurried to his boardinghouse and bound up the wound, relieved to find it had not touched the bone. Of course Fritz Benner would be furious. Well, to hell with him. Benner could have gotten him killed!

He would tell Benner the two men had left the city—whether it was true or not.

And someone else could go after them.

Chapter Four

THEY crossed the Mississippi River on a wide, flat barge and had a three-hour layover at a crossroads burg named Butler, on account of a shattered wheel.

The town had a telegraph office, and Laredo composed a wire to John Fleming, telling him the details of the fight with Amend and the bearded man, asking if Fleming could trace Amend—if Amend had pals, for instance, who might turn up in their future. He described the man who'd gotten away.

He had few hopes that Fleming would be able to discover the bearded man's name, and he was astonished when he received a return wire. William Amend had worked with a man named Erich Ganz, according to police reports, and Ganz was known to have a connection to Fritz Benner. Had Benner's name turned up?

Laredo reported it had not.

A police description of Ganz matched that of the sketch the night clerk had made for them. Ganz was described as being very dangerous, a killer in fact. He was suspected of being involved in the deaths of several persons and was wanted for questioning by several law enforcement agencies.

The wheel fixed, they went on, rolling into Kansas City eight and a half days after leaving Chicago. They rented rooms in the first hotel they came to, soaped themselves in tubs of hot water, and fell into beds to sleep for hours, still feeling the jolting of the unsprung stagecoach.

The next day they bought tickets on the Union Pacific, boarded the train, and rode to Denver—a mile high, the signs said.

The Denver newspapers had carried a small item about a man's body being found in a park in Chicago. The body was still unidentified and the killers were said to be two men who were seen leaving the park. No arrests had been made.

"What about this man Ganz?" Pete asked. "I wonder if he will follow us."

"He may, if he knows about the shipment."

"So he may turn up in Carson City."

Laredo shrugged. "Unless he shaves that beard we'll know 'im."

"I think you hit him in the park. No telling how bad it is. He may be home in bed."

"Yes. But if he's following us, we'll know him and he will know us."

They took the train to Cheyenne and changed to the Southern Pacific for the ride to Carson City. They arrived at night and registered at the nearest hotel without seeing any sign of Ganz.

Early the next morning they walked to Doyle Reinhardt's office in the Franklin Building. Reinhardt, in charge of the office—and the area—was expecting them. John Fleming had wired him long since.

Reinhardt was a pleasant-looking man, slightly rotund; he wore thick glasses and had gray hair. He had been an investigator for the department for many years and was now thankful to sit at a desk and let the younger men sleep on the ground and ride around in the rain.

26

He ushered them in and asked them to be seated, offering them coffee. "I'm damned glad to see you. John Fleming thinks highly of you two."

Laredo smiled. "We like John too—except for his cigars."

"Yes, I've heard about them."

Pete asked, "What about the shipment?"

Reinhardt sighed. "Agent Quinlan is in charge of it. Right now the box is in the big safe. Quinlan's supposed to put it on the train—far as I know."

"We're supposed to help guard it," Laredo said.

"Knowing Quinlan," Reinhardt replied, "he won't let you. Just between us, I wouldn't let him guard a jar of pickles, but the Big Brains in Washington don't agree with me."

Pete asked, "Then what do we do?"

Reinhardt shook his head. "If I were you, I'd go down to the Alamo Saloon and have a drink."

Treasury Agent Howard Wehr was not a drinking man. But on this day he was celebrating two important events at one time. Two things had happened on the same day. One was the anniversary of his divorce from a miserable wife, the other his daughter's marriage in Cincinnati.

He had received a telegram of her nuptials and had gone at once to the nearest saloon to toast the lovely bride, and to regret not being there to give her away.

But he had drunk too much too quickly. He was sodden. He lolled in a chair by the wall and cried unashamedly, saying her name over and over again, telling all who would listen that his little girl was being married thousands of miles away, and how happy he was for her—but here he was, guarding a goddam shipment.

Frank Slater heard him say it. And his ears perked up.

Slater had heard the tall man mumbling for an hour, and this was the first interesting thing he'd uttered.

Slater slid into a chair beside Wehr and asked him, "What shipment?"

Wehr gazed at him, seeing only a blur. "Can' tell you. S'a secret."

"Hell, I know lots of secrets."

Wehr nodded. He did too. "Lotsa secrets. A million of 'em." Wehr started laughing. "A million of 'em . . ." That was funny as hell, a million dollars and a million secrets.

Slater had a time calming him down. Wehr would break into giggles. Slater asked, "The shipment's worth a million dollars?"

"Shhhhhh!" Wehr said. "Can' tell nobody that."

Slater got up and looked around for Shorty. He found him snickering with a saloon girl and pulled him away. "Come and help me get this bird outa here."

"What for?"

Slater said to a bartender, "We going to take 'im home. Poor fool's too drunk to walk."

The bar man nodded and paid no attention; it happened all the time.

Slater said to Shorty, "Come on, grab 'is arms." They half carried the drunk outside.

Shorty was a tall man, well over six feet. When they got outside in the night air he said, "What the hell you draggin' him out here for?"

"Because he knows something."

"What?"

"A shipment," Slater said, looking around. Where the hell would they take the drunk? There was an old barn not too far behind the saloon. That might do fine.

"A shipment of what?"

"For crissakes, if I knew what I wouldn't be packin' this drunk around, would I?" He pointed. "Le's take 'im around to the barn."

Shorty grumbled, but he grabbed Wehr's arms and the two of them stumbled off. It was late and there was no one on the street to watch. Most folks were home in bed or in some saloon, getting drunk as God intended.

It took five minutes to walk to the barn through the dry weeds. One door was hanging open, and inside it smelled

28

like animals had been using it, especially a skunk.

They dropped the drunk on a pile of old straw. He collapsed like a half-filled sack of corn and began to snore.

Slater stood over him and shook his head. "What's the best way to squeeze something outa a drunk like him?"

"Jesus, you gotta sober him up first. He don't look like no cowhand. Who is he anyways?"

"I dunno. Never saw him before. Scratch a match, Shorty." Slater squatted and began to go through the drunk's pockets. He came across a wallet. Inside were some papers. Shorty held the match closer.

Slater read the papers and looked around in surprise. "His name's Howard Wehr and he's a goddamn Treasury agent!"

"That's why he knows about a shipment."

"Yeh." Slater rose and stared down at the snoring man. "What the hell kind of a shipment is it, huh?" He looked at Shorty. "A million dollars he said."

"Maybe something going out on the train."

"Yeh. I bet that's it. Jesus! A million dollars! Is there that much money in the world?"

"They'll have a goddam flock of guards then."

Slater nodded, wild thoughts coursing through his head. He might derail the train—hope to get at the shipment that way. Where did they put a shipment like that? He had no idea.

"Not a good bet, me 'n' you going up against a whole passel of guards."

Slater looked at him. That was right. He frowned. "Maybe we oughta cut Turk in. What you figger?"

"Turk?"

"Yeah. He can handle a gun pretty good. We'd need another gun."

"Yeh, maybe we oughta." Shorty pulled at his lower lip.

"All right, I'll stay here with the drunk. You go get Turk. And don't say nothing to anybody but him." He pulled out the makin's and began to roll a cigarette.

Shorty grunted and left. Turk was probably at the Bird

Cage at the other end of town. They had some girl dancers there and Turk liked to watch them. Said it rested his eyes.

When Shorty disappeared in the gloom, Slater searched the drunk again and pocketed the bills and coins he found. Was it really a million-dollar shipment? A man that drunk wouldn't know how to lie, would he? Maybe this was Slater's lucky night. He had never had a wad of money in his life. He had no special talent or skill, and he was old enough to begin to realize he would never be rich. He would scratch for money the rest of his life—unless this panned out.

He sat and stared at the sodden man for an hour, until Shorty and Turk appeared, his thoughts occupied with ways to spend money.

Turk Jessop was a big, burly man, not as tall as Shorty but a good deal bigger than Slater. He was an ex-miner and ex-holdup man. He had spent several years behind bars for relieving citizens of their valuables. But despite that travail, he still found it easier to hold up folks than work. At the moment he was in the chips, but he was always looking for opportunities to use his know-how with a pistol. A man was a fool to pass up a good chance.

So when Shorty told him about what the drunk had said, he was eager to learn more. He hooked up his buckboard and they drove to the old barn. It was midnight by his watch.

The drunken Treasury agent was still snoring. Frank Slater quickly outlined what he had heard and what he suspected. Turk suggested they build a small fire inside the barn where it could not be seen by anyone passing by.

When the fire was a bed of glowing coals, they took off the agent's boots and shook him awake. He had sobered slightly, enough to be surprised at his whereabouts and at the three hard-faced men before him.

Turk got the agent's attention and said pleasantly, "Tell us about the shipment."

"What shipment?"

Turk motioned, and both Slater and Shorty grabbed the

30

man and shoved one bare foot into the coals. The man screamed, and Turk slashed at his face with the back of his huge hand. "Shut up!"

Wehr whimpered, much soberer all of a sudden, "What you want, anyway?"

"Tell us about the shipment."

"I don't know—"

Turk lunged and shoved the burned foot back into the coals. He held it there a moment as Wehr screamed in agony. The smell of burning flesh filled the barn.

"Tell us about the shipment," Turk persisted. "Or you lose a foot."

The agent caved in. "It's going to Washington, D.C., by train. I dunno when—I mean I don't know the exact date."

"What is it?"

"It's a metal box full of valuables. They tell me it's worth a couple of million." Wehr held his foot, moaning.

"Where is it now?"

"Quinlan put it in the big office safe."

"Who's Quinlan?"

"The agent in charge."

"Where is he?"

"He's staying at the Rossi Hotel." Wehr could barely get the words out.

Turk asked, "When is it going to be put on the train?"

"I told you, I don't know. It's not my decision. It's Quinlan's."

"How many agents are guarding it?"

"Five."

"Counting you?"

"No. Six with me."

Turk rose and walked away from the fire. Frank Slater joined him and they walked to the door of the barn as Shorty gazed after them. "Six agents," Turk said. "Damn. That's too many. You figger he's tellin' the truth?"

"I dunno. But that's about all he knows."

"Yeh. Guess it is." Turk took out his pistol and looked

31

at the loads. "I got an old blanket in the wagon. You wanna go get it?"

"All right." Slater walked into the darkness.

Turk pulled back the hammer of the pistol and walked back to the fire. He stopped behind Wehr—and shot him in the back of the head.

Shorty and Slater were both startled, not having figured on murder. Slater ran back with the blanket. "What you do that for?"

Turk said, "You gonna let him go? He seen you and me and Shorty." Turk pushed out the brass and reloaded. He slid the pistol into his belt. "Wrap 'im in the blanket and put 'im in the wagon."

Slater said, "Where the hell you gonna take 'im?"

"Out in the sticks and bury 'im."

Shorty said, "I don't like this none. . . . You shoulda asked us, Turk."

Turk growled at him. "Put 'im in the goddam wagon."

Slater blew out his breath. He went to the wagon and dropped the tailgate. Then he and Shorty lifted the body in. Turk walked out to the street as they did it, looking around. If anyone had heard the shot they weren't curious.

He went back and they climbed in the wagon and drove away from the old barn.

Shorty said, "We ain't got a shovel."

"There's one in the wagon," Turk replied. "Allus carry it."

Turk drove past the last houses, into the open prairie. The light wagon bounced over the sod, rattling and squeaking. Turk chewed on a cigar and drove for several miles, finally halting near a narrow dry wash.

He pointed. "Right over there's a good place. Right by them rocks."

Shorty got down with the shovel and began to dig.

Slater spelled Shorty with the shovel; the digging was easy and it went rapidly. Turk did no digging. He paced back and forth, staring out over the empty prairie as the others worked. When they were four feet down, Turk growled that it was deep enough.

They pulled the body out of the wagon and rolled it into the ragged hole. Slater shoveled in the dirt; now and then Shorty pounded the dirt down with his boot heels.

When the hole was filled, they scattered twigs and pebbles over it. Then they got in the wagon and drove back to town.

Chapter Five

DOYLE Reinhardt had sources. He never called them informers. Before joining the Treasury Department as an investigator, he had been a policeman in Maryland. In Carson City he kept his ear to the ground. He paid several "sources" for information, and the information was often good.

Almost immediately he heard about Turk Jessop. The day after Howard Wehr had disappeared, Reinhardt had information that two men, Frank Slater and Shorty, had helped him from a saloon. The two men were associates of Jessop. Turk Jessop was a very shady character. Reinhardt was willing to lay almost any crime at his door.

He called in Laredo and Pete Torres to tell them what he had learned. "I suspect they're holding Howard somewhere, to sweat information out of him about the shipment."

"Does Wehr know about it?"

"Yes, he does. He's one of Quinlan's group."

Pete asked, "How would anyone know about the shipment in the first place?"

"We try like hell to keep things secret," Reinhardt said, "but they get out. The bartender tells me that Howard had been drinking heavily and talking about his daughter's marriage, to anyone who would listen."

"Was he a drinker?"

"No, I'm told he seldom drinks. That's what worries me. A man who doesn't drink could get drunk and not realize it. Then he's liable to say anything. The bartender said he only heard Howard talk about his daughter, but that doesn't mean he couldn't have said something about the shipment." He shook his head. "And Turk Jessop is the kind of man who would get the rest out of him."

"What does Jessop look like?"

"He's a big man, big as Pete here. Quick with a gun. He often hangs out at the Bird Cage Saloon, but he knows every low-life in this part of the country."

Laredo looked at Pete. "Let's pay a visit to the Bird Cage." He went to the door, paused, and came back, rubbing his chin. To Reinhardt he said, "Ask around about Slater and Shorty too—where they live. This doesn't listen well at all."

Pete said, "If they've taken Wehr, how can they let him go? He can identify them."

"Shit," Reinhardt said. "All right, I'll get on it."

The Bird Cage Saloon was a deadfall. It was almost deserted in the morning, one barman on duty. No, he hadn't seen Turk Jessop. "You friends o' his'n?"

"Friends of the family," Laredo said. "We just up from Oklahoma. He got an uncle there, you know."

"Turk tole me he didn't have no relatives atall."

"That so? Well, he does. Where's he live?"

The bartender shook his head. "Don't know."

Pete screwed his face into a scowl, drew his pistol, cocked it, and laid it on the bar, muzzle toward the bartender. "You sure you don't know?"

Laredo said quickly, "Don't get riled, Emilio, this

man's all right." He motioned to the bartender. "Don't rile him, for God's sake!"

The bartender was pale. He pressed against the backbar, mouth open, eyeing the pistol. "I remember him sayin' somethin' about living at the Widow's place."

"Where's that?"

"Next street over, third'r fourth house. They's a sign."

"Thanks, friend." Laredo smiled and Pete picked up the pistol, looking disappointed. They went out to the street.

The barman was right; there was a sign. They rapped on the door and a large woman in a blue dress came to the screen and looked at them.

Laredo asked for Turk Jessop and the woman shook her head. "Ain't seen him since yestiddy."

"He's not here now?"

"Nope. He don't keep reg'lar hours."

"Where d'you think we can find him?"

She pulled her mouth down. "Try the Bird Cage."

Laredo sighed. "Thanks. We will."

They rode back to Reinhardt's office. The agent was pacing the room. "I just got a note from Quinlan. The damn fool is taking the shipment to Reno!"

"Why?"

"I don't know."

Pete asked, "Did Howard Wehr know Quinlan was going to Reno with the box?"

"I don't know if he did or not."

Laredo looked at Pete. "If Jessop got Wehr to tell him about it, then Jessop is after Quinlan, sure as a gun."

Reinhardt sat down, sighing deeply. "The damn shipment's lost. That fool Quinlan has lost it."

Pete asked, "How d'we get to Reno?"

"Only one road," Reinhardt said. "Straight through town."

Gerard Quinlan was a slim, nervous man, quick of speech and animated. His father had been a very highly placed official in the department, and young Gerard bene-

36

fited by those friendships when he joined. In the following years he had moved up rather more rapidly than his brains or performance warranted, and his failures were somehow excused.

His appointment to head the team assigned to bring the shipment to the capital was as unexpected as it was ill-directed.

Quinlan had been assigned three men to help. They were Howard Wehr, John Atwood, and Bert Fortner. All men with more experience than he.

When Howard Wehr did not appear in the morning, Quinlan conferred with Reinhardt and learned about the saloon incident. Two men had helped Wehr out—two men with bad reputations. Since Wehr could not be found, Reinhardt's theory was that he was being squeezed. He would be forced to tell Quinlan's plans for putting the box on the train.

Quinlan then got the wind up. Instead of putting the box on the train, he would take it to Reno; that would put the conspirators completely off the track. Quinlan would then put the box on the train at Reno and all would be well.

When he heard about Turk Jessop, Quinlan was in a panic. The thing to do was get away, get out of Carson City as quickly as possible. His logic, he thought, was incontestable. If the thieves could not find the box, they could not steal it. And he would not listen to either Atwood or Fortner who told him. "They may be watching us! They will only follow us!"

"Not if we're quick!"

He had the box put into a wagon pulled by two mules. They piled into the wagon and set out.

Atwood and Fortner were correct. They were watched and followed. Turk Jessop put field glasses on them. There were only three men on the wagon, not five. Wehr had lied to them. Two men were on the wagon seat, one was in the back with a rifle, sitting beside a square metal box. That must be the shipment containing the million dollars.

37

Turk Jessop made his move when the wagon was about five miles out of town. The rutted road ran along the side of a gentle hill, and as the wagon approached a turn Jessop and his two fired on it, aiming at the mules.

But Atwood, driving the wagon, was quick. Standing, he shouted at the mules and slapped the reins. The wheels turned in the soft dirt, kicking up dust, and the mules broke into a run. In the wagon bed, Fortner fired back, levering the Winchester as fast as he could pull the trigger.

In moments they were out of range, and Fortner reloaded the rifle. "I saw three of them!"

"Did you hit any?"

"I don't know—hard to tell. A hell of a lot of dust . . ." Fortner craned his neck. "You all right?"

Quinlan was scared. Reinhardt had told him there would be three men after them. These were not ordinary holdup men lurking along a road. These men were after the box.

The wagon had been hit twice, but the mules and everyone else was untouched. Atwood kept them at a run for another mile then reined in to walk them, though Quinlan told him to hurry.

"If we run them till they're tired, they'll be no good if we need speed."

"We have to get away from them!" Quinlan reloaded his revolver. He had fired wildly at the attackers, hardly aiming, contributing only to the noise. Damn. If he lost this package, would his powerful friends in Washington be able to go to bat for him? Doyle Reinhardt would certainly testify that he had advised against running to Reno by wagon. . . .

He kept his eyes on the back trail. They would probably be attacked again. He wished he knew the route better.

Atwood said, growling, "We have to follow the damn road. We'd wreck the wagon if we got off it. But those bastards can go anywhere on horseback. They can get in front of us."

"Not if we hurry," Quinlan said.

Fortner glanced around. "What if we turn around and go back? They might not think of that."

"No," Quinlan said stiffly. "We'll go on. We beat 'em off once. We can do it again." He turned his head constantly. "Keep a good lookout."

The second attack came an hour later, from the side. They were crossing a dry creek bed, with towering pines on their right, when Jessop and his men opened up with rifles from a short distance.

Atwood swung the mules around instantly, presenting the bushwhackers the rear end of the wagon. Fortner fired a fusillade, and Quinlan and Fortner jumped to the ground, firing at smoke.

In a few moments the attackers were silent. Atwood said, "You think we hit anybody?"

"Hurry—let's go on," Quinlan said. "Pull the wagon up that slope, John."

"Not for a minute," Atwood replied.

Quinlan looked around. "What's the matter?" Then he saw the mule. One of the team had been drilled through the head and was sprawled in the traces. Atwood jumped down with a knife.

"Shit." Quinlan spat. "Cut 'im loose. We'll have to go on with one."

Atwood severed the lines and climbed back on the seat. But it was awkward driving with one animal. The mule constantly tried to step to the right, and they made slow progress.

The road wound through brush and trees, and suddenly there were shots. Atwood half stood, then fell heavily from the seat. At the same instant the mule bolted and ran off the road into a gulley, turning the wagon over.

Quinlan and Fortner jumped free, ending up in the thick brush. The firing from in front continued, hot and fast, the bullets clipping the bark over them, rapping into trees inches from their heads.

Fortner grabbed Quinlan's leg, hissing, "Slide back—slide—" He pulled at the other. "Into the gulley..."

"We can't leave Johnny!"

"The hell we can't. He's dead!"

Quinlan stared at him from a pale face. "How d'you know?"

"I saw him when he fell. He got one through the forehead."

Quinlan seemed to wilt and Fortner yanked at him. "Come on!"

They gained the gulley; the firing at them continued, lead searching out every inch of the brush they had just left. Somewhere in front of them was the smashed wagon. They heard the mule scream, then it was silent.

He had lost the shipment. To go back for it was certain death. Would they believe that in Washington?

Quinlan heard men calling, probably signaling. A few random shots slammed into the gulley, ricocheting off rocks. Fortner nudged him "Back, crawl back—we gotta get out of here or we're dead."

"We lost the box. . . . "

"To hell with the box. We'll lose more'n that if we don't hustle."

Miserable, feeling dead inside, Quinlan followed the other. He had lost the box. It was all he could think of. He had lost the goddam box. But it wasn't his fault. They should have given him more men. Where the hell was Howard Wehr?

Fortner got to his feet after a bit, and pulled Quinlan up. "Let's go—hurry! They'll be looking for us on horses!"

They ran for half a mile, then Fortner climbed out of the gulley onto a rocky shelf. "Come on. . . . " He ran into the trees; the ground was carpeted with pine needles, a thick cushion.

He motioned to Quinlan. "They won't be able to track us on this."

They had gone only a short distance when Quinlan heard the hoofbeats. Bert was right, they were coming on horseback! He flopped in the brush with Fortner and lay motionless.

The two horses went past them, loping along the gulley.

When the sounds had gone, Bert nudged him. "Let's go." He got to his feet and Quinlan followed, feeling very tired. Where were they going? He ran after Fortner, along a slope under the pines, then up toward a ridge.

After half an hour Fortner halted, peering back the way they had come. "We may have given them the slip—but they'll beat the bushes. How d'you feel?"

"Terrible."

"Yeh, it's no good about Atwood. He was damned unlucky. It could've been either of us—or both." Fortner was a stocky man with a black mustache. He had always before seemed to Quinlan to be a follower, but right now he was a leader, no doubt about it. And for the moment Quinlan was content to let him lead. He couldn't seem to think clearly. A picture of the wagon upside down in the brush bleared his thoughts.

He said to Fortner, "Where are we heading?"

"Back toward the town. We'll have to make a big circle though, and enter it after dark. You feel good enough to go on?"

Quinlan nodded. He had to go on.

"All right. Let's keep moving." Fortner went ahead, climbing the slope doggedly, setting a steady pace.

God, he felt terrible. Not because of John Atwood, but because he had lost the shipment. That was the main thing. Atwood had to take his chances like the rest of them. Quinlan gritted his teeth. He had put in a lot of years in the department. Would they say this was all his fault? Damn them!

It had been no great trick to get ahead of the three men in the wagon. It was pulled by only one mule now, and not going very fast. Jessop watched from a distance, knowing the three were goners. They could not escape him now.

They picked out a good ambush spot and waited, lying on their bellies, chewing grass stems, with rifles pointed

41

down the road. The fools in the wagon would ride right into it, and that would be their finish.

It almost happened that way. When the wagon appeared, they fired. Turk Jessop grinned, levering the Winchester. Dumb as hell, those agents. Didn't know an ambush until they ran smack-dab into it. He saw one agent tumble off the wagon, then the mule ran the rig off the road into the ditch, overturning the wagon. He could see one wheel spinning in the air.

He stopped firing to listen, then motioned the others to keep up a steady fire, searching the bushes.

Slater said finally, "We must have got 'em all. . . ."

"Go down and look then."

They moved slowly to the wagon, rifles ready, but no one was near. A few birds began to gossip high in the pine branches. The agent who had fallen off the wagon was dead, a hole in his forehead. The mule had screamed once and died. The metal box had tumbled into the weeds. Shorty and Slater heaved it up and brought it to the road. Jessop gazed at it fondly.

If what they said was true, it contained millions!

Millions!

Jessop patted the dull metal, and a feeling of elation came over him so strong that he almost smiled. Then he growled at the two, "Get after them others. They musta run along the gulley."

Frank Slater looked at him, then at the box.

Turk said, "You figger I can put this here in my goddam pocket? Get after them before they gets away!"

Shorty and Slater ran for the horses.

Chapter Six

THE Reno road was well traveled and had been graded not long before, so they made good time. Five or six miles from the city Laredo thought he heard gunfire. He reined in. "You hear that?"

Pete cupped a hand behind his ear. "Sounds like a fight." He looked at the blue sky. It was certainly not thunder.

"Now it's stopped. . . ."

They went forward slowly, walking the horses, stopping to listen. The firing had ceased. Had Quinlan and his men gotten into a gunfight?

According to Reinhardt, Quinlan and his group had a wagon. It would be practically impossible for a man to pack the steel box on a horse by himself.

Wary of an ambush, they rode into the trees and dismounted. They selected a copse where they could see the road without being observed.

A half hour passed, and no one had come along the road.

Laredo nudged Pete. "Let's go up the road. If anyone

43

was there, they're probably long gone." He led the horse out to the road, mounted and checked his pistol; Pete did the same. It was not a good idea to rush into someone else's gunfight.... They went forward slowly, and in a mile or so came upon a wrecked wagon. It had overturned in a gulley and lay half-atop a dead mule. The body of the wagon was riddled with bullets.

Nearby was the body of a man who had died violently, a bullet in his forehead. Pockets had been turned out; there was nothing to tell who he had been.

"He's probably one of Quinlan's Treasury agents," Laredo said. "He doesn't have the look of an outlaw."

"You mean the clothes."

"Yes—too well dressed." Laredo sighed. "Well, we've got to take him in. Reinhardt can probably identify him."

"There's no sign of the steel box." Pete walked the area, kicking brush. "Reinhardt was right. They lost it."

"I'd guess that Jessop ambushed them, killed this one, and got away with the box."

"What happened to the other two agents?"

"Good question. Maybe they ducked out."

Laredo studied the encircling trees. "Let's meander around, see if they're lying out there somewhere, shot up."

They spent most of an hour searching for sign and found nothing but the tracks in the gulley. Apparently two horsemen had run along the gulley for a mile or so and returned to the overturned wagon.

All the tracks in the road and around it were confused; it was impossible to tell where the ambushers had gone.

"Maybe the other two got away and are making for the town," Laredo said.

"And Jessop's sitting somewhere counting his money."

They brought the body into town and stopped at the undertaker's establishment on a side street. Rigor had not yet set in. They carried it inside and the undertaker, Mr. Rasor, and an assistant put it on a back room table.

Rasor, a slim, dour-faced man in black vest and pants,

44

peered at the victim's face. "I've seen him afore, but I don't recollect 'is name. Who is he?"

"We don't know," Pete said. "Maybe Reinhardt will know."

Rasor nodded. "I'll send a boy for 'im." He went out to the front.

Doyle Reinhardt showed up in half an hour and instantly identified the body as that of John Atwood. He looked down sorrowfully at the remains on the metal-sheathed table.

"He never knew what hit 'im," Rasor said. "Never felt a thing. The gov'ment paying for the funeral and burying?"

"I'm afraid it'll have to be a plain pine box," Reinhardt replied. "I have no budget for shootings." He sighed deeply. "Do him good. He was a fine man. Let me know when the burying is."

"Will do."

Reinhardt walked out to the street. Pete and Laredo followed and Pete got out the makin's. Laredo said, "They must have the money box."

Reinhardt nodded. "I knew that stupid Quinlan would lose it. You found no sign of him and Bert Fortner?"

"No."

"I told that goddam Quinlan not to run off to Reno. I'm gonna report it that way. I think he panicked. The sonofabitch brought it down on all of us—and got Atwood killed."

Pete scratched a match and lit the brown cigarette.

Reinhardt said, "You got any idea what happened to Quinlan and Bert?"

Laredo shook his head. "They could have gone any direction. The ground was hard, and men on foot would be hard to track, but we think they got away."

"No sign of them being wounded," Pete said.

"Well, let's hope so. Maybe they'll come in tonight." He pulled out a turnip watch and studied it. "I guess now there isn't anything to do but wait."

"Not much," Laredo said. "We can't prove it was Jessop

and those other two who ambushed the wagon. Where would they take the steel box?"

"God knows," Reinhardt said gloomily. "Let's go have a beer."

Both Laredo and Pete Torres had thrived on the rigorous life at the Tanner Training Center at Barksdale in Missouri. Along with weapons and tactics, they learned about emergency medicine, police procedures, horses, basic tracking, and most of all, survival. They were also detectives of the elite Bluestar unit, selected because the qualities they presented in early cases were unusual. Working with another, veteran, agent, Laredo had brought in half a dozen horse thieves, having outthought them when they assumed themselves safe from capture.

Pete had outmaneuvered several bank robbers and driven them into the arms of the peace officers tracking them.

It was the use of brainpower that made the difference. The Tanner Organization stressed brains over guns. Anyone could pull a trigger, but not everyone could use the brains God gave him.

However, each agent had to be expert with rifle and pistol before he was allowed to go into the field. Few were any better than Laredo with a pistol and Pete Torres with a rifle. Pete had a specially worked-over Winchester that was remarkably accurate at long distances.

Gerard Quinlan and Bert Fortner plodded into town well after dark, after hiding more than ten miles up and down hills to make sure they approached civilization far from the Reno road. They were both exhausted, hungry, and out of sorts.

The Treasury Office was closed so they went to the Rossi Hotel. Quinlan got a bath and slept like one dead, with half a bottle of whiskey inside him to help forget the ambush. He had thought over every excuse he could devise, to make the loss seem like pure circumstance—certainly not his fault. He hadn't had enough men, and the ambushers should be blamed, not he.

Of course it had been Bert Fortner who had insisted they crawl away from the shipment box, into the gulley where they could never reach it.

If they had rescued the steel box . . .

He turned his mind away from the fact that they might well have been killed trying to reach it. But Fortner had pulled him, physically pulled him away!

And as far as the ambush itself was concerned, how in the world could he have known that the thieves were waiting for him? People were robbed every day, and if they could avoid it they certainly would!

His excuses began to sound more plausible the more he drank.

But in spite of everything they had lost the goddam box.

Bert Fortner had a bath also and put on clean clothes. He made notes for his report in the morning to Reinhardt, then he went downstairs and into the nearest saloon to order a beer. He took it to a corner table away from other people.

He knew Quinlan well enough to be sure that Quinlan would blame him for a good part of the debacle but probably use John Atwood as the biggest scapegoat—because Atwood was dead and could not refute him. Quinlan was the poorest excuse for an agent he had ever seen.

The best thing for him to do was ask for a transfer.

He was debating this with himself when Doyle Reinhardt and two other men came into the saloon.

Fortner waved and Reinhardt saw him at once. He and his friends ordered beer and came across to the table.

"Your office was closed," Fortner said.

"God, I'm glad to see you!" Reinhardt looked very relieved. They shook hands. "Thank God you're all right." He sat down. "Where's Quinlan?"

"In his room. He said he had to make out a report that would take him hours. He wanted to do it while it was all fresh in his mind."

"Yes. I'll be glad to read that." Reinhardt made the introductions. Laredo was a tawny-haired man with a pleasant smile and shoulders like a wrestler. Torres was as big, maybe even slightly larger, obviously Hispanic, and moved like a cat.

Both men, Reinhardt told Fortner, worked for the Tanner Organization. They were here in Carson City because of the shipment, taking their instructions through John Fleming's section.

Reinhardt asked, "How did you get away?"

"We were ambushed and Johnny Atwood was hit right away. . . ."

"We saw his body earlier," Reinhardt said. "These two brought him in."

"We were at the spot a while after the fight," Laredo told him. "I don't see how you got out with your lives."

Fortner sighed deeply. "We couldn't reach Johnny or the steel box. We slid into the gulley and managed to crawl down it till we could get into the woods. There was no way we could have reached the box alive. They kept up a murderous fire, trying to locate us. . . ."

"I'd appreciate your report on it," Reinhardt said. "In writing." He sipped beer. "How did Quinlan act?"

"I've already made some notes. We were both scared. It was a harrowing time—for a while I didn't think we'd make it out. I guess we had some luck." Fortner shook his head. "But the box is lost."

"We'll try to get it back." Laredo smiled.

"They'll play hell opening it," Fortner said with a small grin. "It's hardened steel, with a special lock. About the best thing they could do with it is to use it as a stool."

Turk Jessop was delighted to get his hands on the shipment box—until he examined it. The damned thing looked impervious. It was obviously steel, dull finish, no sharp corners, and the lock was curious. It was sunken and narrow, barely a slit. Probably some new invention. He'd never seen anything just like it before.

He searched the body of the dead agent and found nothing that looked like a key. Maybe one of the two who'd gotten away had it. The thing was heavy too. When he picked it up, nothing rattled inside it. It was like a solid chunk of metal. Jessop kicked it, then sat on it, annoyed. How the hell would he get it open?

Slater and Shorty returned, having had no luck, Slater said. The two had given them the slip. There were a million places to hide—especially for men on foot.

"If we camped here and made a systematic search," Slater said, "we could maybe turn 'em up."

It was tempting, in view of the fact that one of them probably had the key—but it was also dangerous. The two might still give them the slip and bring the law back. He didn't want to fool with a posse.

"Let's get out of here."

It was a difficult chore, carrying the awkward steel box. They balanced it on a saddle, and with one man on either side of the horse managed to walk away with it, very slowly.

They followed the road until they could step off it on a rocky area, leaving no tracks. And it took forever to get to the hideout on Hermit Mountain. It was full dark when they finally arrived.

The hideout was a cleverly concealed cabin made of logs with the bark still on them, placed in a copse of trees in a hollow where tall brush was thick.

Almost no one ever came to Hermit Mountain. Not even hunters; they found it easier to find game on the gentler slopes. When you shot a deer on Hermit, you had to lug the damned thing on your back. . . .

They dropped the box into a corner of the hut and got a fire going. Jessop stared at the box as he ate the dried meat they'd broiled. How the hell would he get what was inside? This was the last thing he'd expected. It was a ring-tailed bitch!

Someone in the goddam government had devised a thief-proof safe. Trust the government to do the wrong

49

thing at the right time. What if he put blasting powder under it? He might blow it open, but what would happen to the insides?

Jesus! He had millions in his grasp, and he could not reach them!

Apparently Shorty and Slater had come to the same conclusion. He saw them staring at him, and finally Frank said, "What the hell we going to do about this here box, Turk? How we gonna open it?"

"We'll open it."

"Yeh? How?"

Jessop had been thinking hard. He nodded sagely. "I know how. How far's Huffield?"

Frank shrugged. "Maybe twenty miles."

Shorty asked, "What's in Huffield? Last time I was there it was a wide place in the goddam road."

"Waco's there."

"Waco?"

Jessop nodded almost amiably. "He's a blacksmith, old friend o'mine. If anybody can get into that damned box, he can." He pulled out a cigar and dusted it off. "Tomorra I ride over to Huffield and talk to Waco. You-all stay here and guard the box."

"That box don't need no guard from nobody," Shorty said. "It's like a chunk of iron."

"Well, guard it anyhow. Soon's we get it open, then the fun begins. We going to be rich."

"*If* we get it open," Slater said morosely.

"We'll get it open," Jessop assured him. But as he drifted off to sleep he was not at all sure—and he didn't want to think farther than that.

In the morning they ate cold beans and hot, bitter coffee, then Jessop climbed on his horse and set off down the mountain to the flats.

He had no worries about leaving the box in their care. They expected him to bring back directions for opening it. That was simpler than trying to find out themselves.

It was a long, dusty ride to Huffield and took the entire

50

day. It was a weather-beaten little town, huddled up against a brushy mountain, that catered mostly to miners. There was copper and silver in the area, damned little gold. Jessop was tired to death when he arrived, crotch-sore and irritable.

Waco wasn't at the blacksmith shop. A boy said he'd gone somewhere or other but would be back the next day —maybe.

He spent the night in the livery stable; there was no hotel in the little burg. He rented a cot from the stable owner and slept in a stall beside his horse. In the cold morning he had beefsteak for breakfast and found a chair in front of the blacksmith shop, waiting for Waco to return.

Waco finally appeared, driving a battered wagon loaded with iron objects that needed repairing. He'd been out rounding up work, he told Jessop. "Man's got to hustle these days to keep eatin'." Waco was a big man, broad and tough as boardinghouse steak. "What you come all the way out here for, Turk?"

"T'see you about a bit of business."

Waco pulled on a leather apron. "All right. What is it?"

"I've got a steel box that needs opening."

"You lost the key?"

"Never did have it. It's a big, heavy bastard." Jessop showed the other with his hands. "About this size. Got a kind of funny lock on her. Think you can burn a hole in it?"

Waco looked around. "You bring it with you?"

"No. Wasn't sure you could do 'er."

"Well, I can probably burn a hole in it, sure. Course it'll take awhile. . . ."

Jessop nodded. "I don't care. Got the time."

"But what about what's inside?" Waco cocked his head at the other. "Ain't that what you want?"

"Yeh . . . sure."

"Well, what's inside is gonna burn too. This thing is a safe, huh?"

"You could call it that. It's a shipment box."

"Sounds to me like what you got is a hardened steel

51

box. Somebody don't want you t'get into it without a key."

"That's right."

"So—if I put enough heat on it to burn a hole, it's gonna burn the insides too."

Jessop sighed deeply. "No way around it?"

"No way I know about." Waco shrugged. "D'you know what's inside?"

"I'm not sure. But paper, for certain."

"Well, if it's paper, forget all about it. If it's metal, it'll puddle. If it's jewels, they're lost." The blacksmith shook his dark head. "If it was me, I wouldn't think of burnin' it."

"All right. Then could you saw into it?"

"No saw made could get into it." Waco made a face. "Well, maybe in four or five hunnerd years . . . usin' ten thousand saw blades."

"What about drills?"

"I ain't got any drill f'that kind of work."

"Who would have one?"

Waco shrugged again. "Maybe somebody in San Francisco. . . ."

Chapter Seven

"**I** HAVE sources," Doyle Reinhardt said. "I had a time convincing my superiors that it would pay off, but it does, so now I have a small budget for them. One came to me last night with some information about Turk Jessop."

"Go on," Laredo said. They were in Reinhardt's office on the second floor, front. The two windows were open and they had a fine view of the broad main street below. Pete sat by one of the windows, blowing smoke out.

Reinhardt smiled. He got up and walked to the window. "I didn't know this before—but then of course I hadn't asked for information on Jessop." He pointed down the street. "See that?"

"What?"

"Across the street. The Paradise."

"The saloon?"

"Yes. It's owned and run by a woman named Maria Colosi. She sings and dances on the stage in the back, along with an ensemble, of course. I've heard her and she's pretty good." He turned and looked at them. "My source tells me she is Jessop's woman friend. Sooner or later he'll show up there to see her—or at her house."

Pete asked, "Are they married?"

"No. She's widowed. She's in her thirties, I'd say. Her husband left her the saloon and the house. Nice-looking woman. Dunno what she sees in Jessop."

"Women are strange," Pete said, staring at the street. "A lot of them make eyes at Laredo."

Reinhardt laughed. "Can't imagine it. Well, anyway, they tell me Jessop is a jealous type. There've been quite a few fights in the Paradise because some gent pinched Maria's bottom."

Laredo nodded. "So you think he won't stay away long?"

"That's right. He'll want to make sure she's not seeing someone else." Reinhardt went back to his desk and sat down. "And my source tells me—she is. He says she is about through with Jessop. He's too goddam possessive."

"D'you think we can talk to her?"

"I'm sure you can."

"When does the Paradise open?"

Reinhardt looked at his turnip watch. "It's open now, but Maria won't be there yet. They tell me she never shows up till about midday. The saloon closes late, you know."

Laredo grinned at Pete. "Let's go have a beer. . . . "

They waited till noon, then walked down the street and into the saloon–dance hall. It was nearly deserted at that hour. A single man, a miner by the look of him, was sipping a stein at one end of the bar. A neatly combed man in a fresh white apron was talking to a woman at the other end. They seemed to be discussing papers and a ledger.

The room was warm and high-ceilinged, almost cavernous. To the left was a wide door opening onto a huge room that, early in the day, was unlit and appeared gloomy. It must be the dance hall, Laredo thought.

The woman was dressed in a purplish gown with much white lace about the neck and high sleeves. Rings flashed on her fingers. This had to be Maria Colosi. She glanced around at them as they entered, then turned her back, continuing to talk with the barman. She was making notes on a sheet of paper and showing them now and then to her companion. Once or twice the bartender took a bottle from the backbar and they discussed it for a moment, then he put it back.

Laredo and Pete leaned against the bar, a dozen or more feet from the pair, and Pete clinked a coin on the polished wood. The bartender looked up, said something to the woman, put down his pencil and came toward them.

"What'll it be, gents?"

"Beer," Laredo said and Pete nodded.

The barman drew the two beers.

Laredo said to the woman, "You Miss Colosi, ma'am?"

She turned with the ghost of a smile. "Yes . . ."

"Like to talk to you a minute—matter of business."

She was not enthused. "What kind of business, please?"

"About Turk Jessop."

She stared at him, looked at Pete, and frowned. Laredo smiled. "It won't take long."

In a moment she sighed. "Very well." She spoke a few words to the bartender and folded the ledger. "Come this way then."

She walked toward the back, past a piano and tables, and opened a hall door. It was a small, busy-looking office with papers strewn over a desk. She tidied it as Laredo and Pete entered and found chairs. Then she sat behind the desk. "All right. What's it about?"

Laredo said, "Jessop's on the run from the law."

"That's nothing new." She opened a drawer and rummaged in it, bringing out a thin black cheroot. She eyed them both. "Are you lawmen?"

"In a way."

Scratching a match, she lit the cheroot. Pete's eyes widened. He had never seen a woman smoke a cigar before and it fascinated him.

"Why do you come to me?"

"We were told you and Jessop were very close."

55

She blew smoke toward the ceiling. "Gossip. We are *not* very close—whatever that means."

"But you were?..."

"A time ago, yes. Not anymore."

Up close, Laredo thought she was probably slightly older than Reinhardt had said. The wrinkles probably did not show from the stage where she performed.

She asked, "What's he done?"

"Stolen a shipment from the Treasury Department."

"Treasury?..." She looked interested. "You mean money?"

"Money and other valuables amounting to quite a bit. When did you last see him?"

She looked at a point between them. "Oh, perhaps a week ago. He was in the saloon. Came in for a drink and left right away. We didn't speak."

Pete asked, "Do you expect him back?"

Her eyes blazed for a moment. "I hope not! I don't want anything to do with him, the sonofabitch! The last time I talked to him I told him to stay away."

Laredo studied her. Was this an act or not? She was a performer, after all.

She seemed to divine his thoughts. Suddenly she pulled the strap off her shoulder, pushing the purple dress down. Her ivory skin was mottled an ugly yellow and brown. "He beats me," she said. "That's why." She pulled the dress up again. "Now I can't wear half my clothes or the bruises show."

Laredo nodded. That pretty much settled his wondering.

Pete asked, "Have you any idea where we can find him?"

"No." She puffed furiously on the cheroot. "Do you know Shorty and Frank Slater?"

"We know about them, yes."

"They sometimes hang out with Turk—especially Frank. Find him and you might find Turk."

"Do those two come in here?"

She shrugged. "I expect so. We put on the best show in

56

town. I don't see all the people who come in, of course. That would be impossible."

"I suppose so," Laredo agreed. "But you don't *expect* Jessop to show up?"

"No, I don't."

"What about Shorty? Do you know where he lives?"

"All I know is that he sometimes stays with Carl Smith. He's a carpenter. I believe they call him Smitty. You'll find him near the end of town. There's a sign out front."

"Is Shorty a carpenter?"

"I don't know." She looked at the cigar. "I think he helps Carl out for room and board. That's my suspicion, mostly. I heard Turk send a boy for him once. . . . ."

Pete said, "If you see or hear from Turk will you let us know? You can reach us through Doyle Reinhardt."

She nodded. "Yeh, I will."

They got up to go and Laredo said, "Thank you very much, Miss Colosi. You've been very helpful. We'll keep all this under our hats."

She smiled. "Watch your backs. Turk—he's a back-shooter."

Pete nodded. "Thanks."

They mounted their horses, rode toward the end of town, and found Smitty's sign: CARL SMITH, CARPENTER. It was hand-painted but legible.

Smitty was home. He was in the shop at the side of the house. It was a large, lean-to building with small windows, and smelled of sawdust inside. Smitty was a chunky man with large hands and sparse blond hair. He wore steel-rimmed glasses and was planing some long boards when they stopped in the door.

He squinted at them, took off the glasses, and wiped his eyes. "What can I do for you, gents?"

Laredo said hello. "Nice place you have here. Is Shorty around?"

"Haven't seen him."

"We're told he works for you and stays here."

57

"What you want with Shorty?"

"Want to talk to him."

"You lawmen?"

"Why? Has Shorty been in trouble with the law before?"

Smitty put the glasses back on. "You look like lawmen."

"That so? Does Shorty work for you? Does he stay here?" Laredo and Pete entered the shop, separating so they had Smitty between them. He looked from one to the other, frowning.

"He don't stay here no more."

"When did you see him last?"

Smitty pursed his thin lips. "Three, four days ago maybe. What's he done?"

"You know Frank Slater?"

"Sure. Ever'body in town knows Frank."

"Why did Shorty leave here?"

"How d'I know? He just up and left. What'd he do?"

"Murder and robbery."

"Jesus! Him and Frank Slater?"

"Yes, and Turk Jessop."

Smitty sat down abruptly, obviously astonished. "Turk too?"

Laredo nodded. "What can you tell us about any of those three?"

"I dunno. Shorty, he stayed here for a spell. Did me some odd jobs for 'is keep. I only see Frank once in a while, and Turk too. Used to see Turk over at the Paradise."

Smitty did not impress Laredo as a man who revered the truth. But he promised to get in touch with them through Doyle Reinhardt if he ran across any of the three.

When they left the shop Pete said, "He'll never tell us a thing."

"I think you're right." They mounted and looked along the street. Pete rolled a cigarette. Laredo said, "Maybe our best bet is to watch Maria Colosi—see if Jessop shows up.

Jessop is more likely to go after her than Smitty is to see Shorty. What d'you think?"

"Well, she's a good-looking woman. I'll bet there isn't another one in this town as pretty."

Laredo grinned. "Or who smokes cigars."

In the middle of the afternoon they went back to Doyle Reinhardt's office. He was relieved to see them—had been about to go looking for them, he said. "I got a note from Turk Jessop little bit ago. It came from a young kid who got it from a horseman just outside town." He handed it to them.

> I got your box. You give me one
> million in cash and I will not blast
> it open. If you do not, you will not
> see the box again.

"A ransom note!" Laredo exclaimed.

"I told you," Pete said. "He can't open it."

Reinhardt nodded in agreement. "So he's willing to give it back to us. Very nice of him."

Pete asked, "How d'we contact him?"

"The boy told me Jessop wants an answer. The weekly comes out tomorrow. He wants us to put the answer in the agony column and he'll see it in the next few days. We're to sign it 'Rainbow.'"

"'Rainbow'?"

"That's so it'll be different, I suppose. Then he'll know it's from us." Reinhardt sat behind his desk and frowned at the note. "I already talked to the newspaper editor. It's too late to get an answer in this week's paper."

Laredo shrugged. "He ought to know you haven't the authority to give anyone a million dollars."

"I guess so. . . ."

"So put the answer in next week's edition."

They told the agent about seeing Maria and Smitty, and

that Maria might be telling the truth. They had large doubts about Smitty.

"Don't know 'im," Reinhardt said.

"Maria seems to hate Jessop pretty good," Laredo went on. "She showed us some nasty marks where he beat her, so that's good evidence. We're going to stake her out. Jessop may show up. . . . "

Reinhardt considered it. "I'd stake out her home if I were you. He may not want to show his face in public."

Pete asked, "You know where she lives?"

"Yes. She owns a house not far from the saloon. I'm told she lives with a housekeeper. I can see Jessop going there without any worries about being seen. I'll show you the house after supper tonight when it's dark."

Laredo and Pete had supper in a restaurant, lingered over coffee, and when it was full dark met Reinhardt in front of his office. The agent was smoking a cigar, waiting for them. They walked to Maria's house.

It was a frame building painted brown, the largest in a row of separate houses, fourth from the main street.

"There's a stable behind the house on an alley," the agent said. "If Jessop shows he'll probably come that way."

Laredo nodded. "We'll wait for him in the stable."

They waited only two hours, then went back to the saloon and found Gerard Quinlan there. He was sitting by himself, a bottle in front of him, and he growled at them when they sat down.

"What d'you two want?"

"We'd like to ask you about the shipment box."

"I've nothing to say to you. That is government business. I cannot discuss it."

"Did you see any of the men who fired on you?"

Quinlan turned angrily. "I told you. I have nothing to say to you!"

Laredo said, "How about talking about John Atwood?"

Quinlan jumped up, knocking his chair over. He shouted, "I have nothing to say to you!" He hurried out to the street.

They watched him go and Pete said, "He knows he killed Atwood."

Chapter Eight

In Washington, D.C., John Fleming had instituted a quiet investigation to determine where the leak came from. His two agents, Laredo and Torres, had been followed in Chicago when the case was barely two days old. There had been a gunfight and one man, Will Amend, was dead.

Amend led them to Erich Ganz, and from Ganz to Fritz Benner. Did Benner pay Ganz and Amend to shadow the agents?

If so, how did Benner know about the shipment? That was the big question. Benner had been shadowed and tailed but so far nothing had been discovered. None of the people he talked to was on the confidential list of government personnel who knew about the steel box.

The investigation was digging deeper. There had been a leak. It had to be found.

Another telegram came to John Fleming from Doyle Reinhardt in Nevada. Fleming chewed his cigar as he read it. The steel shipment box had been lost by Gerard Quinlan's stupidity.

"Of course he lost it," Fleming said aloud, to an empty room. "I told them he would."

One man, John Atwood, was dead too, blood on Quinlan's hands. Reinhardt pulled no punches. Quinlan had acted stupidly and had caused Atwood's death. He had acted after he had been well advised—he chose to ignore the good advice.

Reinhardt also thanked Fleming for his foresight in sending Laredo and Torres. "At least we have two good men on the spot very quickly."

Reinhardt also knew who had taken the box; three men: Turk Jessop, Frank Slater, and a man called Shorty. There were of course no witnesses, but overwhelming circumstantial evidence pointed to the three. Fleming could feel the anger in Reinhardt's wire, though the man was thousands of miles away. Fleming clenched his teeth. God, he hoped this would end Quinlan's career!

Fleming sent a wire at once to Reinhardt, asking how Jessop and the others had known about the shipment. They had to know about it to steal it. . . . Or had it been unplanned?

"It was planned," Reinhardt wired back. A Treasury agent, Howard Wehr, was missing. They were of the opinion, in Carson City, that Wehr had been kidnapped and forced to talk. There was no other reasonable explanation. Reinhardt wired that he was much afraid Howard Wehr was dead. "He is probably buried somewhere in the hills and the body will never be found."

Reinhardt also included in that wire the news that a note had been received from Jessop demanding payment of one million dollars, or the steel box would be destroyed.

Fleming swore, puffing smoke. In a way, Reinhardt was passing the buck to him . . . although he did not ask that the ransom be paid. Well, the only thing he could do now that he had been notified was to pass it on upstairs—though he was positive of the answer.

Tucking Reinhardt's wire in his pocket, Fleming went out and down the hall. He climbed two flights of stairs and went into Daniel Humer's office. He spoke briefly to Humer's secretary, a dusty-gray older man with thick spectacles and white hair. He waited while the old man went into the inner office and returned, leaving the door open.

"Please go in, Mr. Fleming."

Daniel Humer was sixtyish, gray and dignified, carefully dressed, with sideburns in a long-past style. He rose as Fleming entered.

"Hello, John. Is it something important?"

"It's about the shipment from Carson City."

"Oh dear. You don't look happy. . . ."

"Yes. I'm afraid something's happened to it."

Humer frowned. "Your memo said you'd dispatched two of Tanner's best men to handle it."

"I did. But the shipment was lost before they arrived on the scene." Fleming filled his superior in on the circumstances, as Humer clucked his tongue. Fleming presented the telegrams and puffed his cigar as Humer read them.

Humer shook his head definitely. "No. We cannot start this. There will be no payments of that kind while I am head of this department. Every crook and thief in America would be holding us up for ransom if we did. No. I absolutely forbid it."

"Good. That's what I was sure you'd say." Fleming went to the door. "I'll get a wire off to Reinhardt on that score at once."

Humer nodded. "Keep me posted, John." He watched the other go out and close the door. Then he hurried to open both his windows and fanned the smoke with a newspaper.

A young lad delivered an envelope to Doyle Reinhardt's office, addressed to Laredo Garrett. Reinhardt gave the lad a half dime to take it to the Rossi Hotel and hand it personally to Laredo.

The boy said nothing about receiving a coin from Reinhardt and Laredo absently gave him another. The lad went off whistling.

It was a note from Maria Colosi asking him to call upon her at home. She had remembered something that might help the investigation. The note provided directions to her home—she did not know he already knew where it was. He and Pete went there at once.

She met them at the door herself. She was dressed in a flowered housedress, with her hair piled high on her handsome head. She had obviously just gotten out of bed. She led them into the parlor and they sat facing her as she stood in front of the fireplace. Most of the shades were drawn and the room was dim. Maria was not used to sunlight, Laredo thought. He watched her light a thin cheroot as they settled themselves.

She said, "I remembered something Turk told me once. I'm sure he has forgotten he said it. He mentioned it in passing and we never discussed it or brought it up again."

"What is it?"

"He's got a hideout cabin in the hills."

Laredo smiled and glanced at Pete. This was the kind of information they wanted.

"Where is it?"

"It's somewhere on Hermit Mountain—I think in one of the canyons."

"Is it an actual cabin? Not just a cave?"

"It's a cabin, I'm sure. He said he stocked it in case things got too hot for him. He could lie up there for a week or so."

Pete asked, "Can you pinpoint it a little closer?"

"I'm afraid not. I was never there of course. But is it any help?"

"A great deal. Thank you."

Pete asked, "You haven't seen Jessop—since we talked to you?"

"No. I'd have told you at once." She hugged herself. "I'm afraid of him. He's a very violent man. He told me once when he was angry that he'd killed several men. So please be careful."

"We certainly will be," Laredo assured her.

They returned to Reinhardt's office and asked for a map of the area. "We don't have any very good ones," the Treasury man said. "Not much of the wilds has been surveyed." He looked over a stock and pulled out one, spreading it on a table. "This one shows roads and towns, and that's about all. And I'm sure that the placement is guesswork."

"She said Hermit Mountain. . . . "

Reinhardt put his finger down, north of the city. "Here it is. Not a very big range, as you can see. Did she have any idea where the hideout would be?"

"No. None."

Pete said, "The map doesn't show any roads into that area. Is that accurate?"

"Yes. There are none. But I'm sure there are trails. I mean a horse could go there with no trouble, but not a wagon."

Laredo looked at Pete. "Well, we can ride around a bit and see what we can scare up. . . . Maybe we'll find a trail to lead us somewhere."

"Good luck."

Pete asked, "Did you put the reply in the agony column?"

Reinhardt nodded. "It'll be in this issue. If the press hasn't broken down again."

"That means Jessop is staying around to read it, huh?"

"I'd think so."

The weather was holding, bright and sunny in the daytime and slightly misty at night, as autumn approached on her stealthy feet. With full canteens and food in gunny sacks, Laredo and Pete left the town after dark and headed north.

There was no trail to Hermit Mountain. According to Reinhardt, they would have to go across country by dead reckoning. And it might be difficult to tell when they got there. One mountain looked very like another. Jessop's hideaway cabin was undoubtedly camouflaged. They might have to be almost on top of it before they saw it.

It was very like searching for a needle in a field of bean sprouts. But it had to be done. As Pete said, they might get lucky.

Halting ten miles or so out of town, they made a cold camp and slept till sun-up. The hills were brown and dusty; Laredo had read somewhere that Nevada had the least rainfall of any state in the Union. Seeing it first hand, he could not quarrel with that.

They went on more slowly, and at the end of the day had what they were sure was Hermit Mountain before them. They camped again without a fire and were up with the sun. Hermit was a rugged-looking range with deep canyons, ideal for a hideout hut. Jessop had chosen well.

"We ought to find the cabin on one of them," Pete said, frowning at a narrow canyon. "If we don't find a bullet first."

That was a definite possibility, an ambush; three rifles against two, and the three well hidden. You never hear the one that hits you, it was said. And they might present a very good target indeed if they approached a hidden cabin.

Laredo had brought along a pair of field glasses borrowed from Reinhardt, and they passed them back and forth, scanning the terrain before going on.

And then, late in the afternoon, when the shadows were long, they came across what might be a trail. Shod horses had passed that way, the shadows making the tracks more obvious.

"They look fresh," Pete thought. "Not a week old . . ."

They picketed the horses well off the trail and went ahead on foot, wary as Apaches.

As darkness closed in, they found the cabin.

It had been cleverly placed in a dense grove of a slender pines, built with barked wood, and none of it was visible from twenty feet. Pete spotted it first because of a coffee tin carelessly dropped in the weeds near the door.

Pete watched the door and Laredo made a circle, looking for horses, and found none.

"There's no one home," he said to Pete.

No one came out and no one went in. When darkness fell, no light came on inside the hut.

But they waited till dawn, then opened the door to find the small cabin empty. There were some airtights on a shelf, a box of stick matches, and some cut wood for a fire.

"No shipment box," Pete said.

"Let's search around the cabin."

They found nothing and were very disappointed. But someone had been in the cabin recently.

"But it could have been anyone. . . . "

Though Turk Jessop was confident no one knew of the hideaway cabin, he did not want to leave the steel box there. They balanced it on a saddle again and carried it several miles away to a well-hidden cave.

"Nobody will ever find it here," Jessop said. "We'll come back for it later."

They rode back to the town and parted outside it, after agreeing to meet in two days at Frank Slater's shack. Jessop would figure out how to get into the box, he told them. There had to be an answer.

Slater and Shorty rode on together and came into the town at evening time. They went by back streets to the shack Slater called home and they tied the horses by the door. The shack was behind a row of empty corn cribs. Slater exchanged work for the use of the shack; the property was owned by a merchant in town, Peter Cutler. Slater chopped firewood for Cutler and repaired fences when they needed it.

The shack wasn't much. It had one room, a puncheon floor, a shedlike slanting roof that leaked when it rained, and one window. There was a rope bed, a single table, and two boxes for chairs. A lantern hung by a wire in the middle of the room over the table. Outside the door was a circle of stones as a fireplace if Slater wanted to cook something. Cutler had promised to get him an iron stove for inside, come next winter.

There was very little food in cans, but there was a half-full bottle of whiskey. Slater got it down and set out two dusty glasses.

"Well, what you figger, Shorty?"

"About the box?"

Slater poured into the two glasses. "Yeah—we do the job, get shot at in the bargain, but there's no payoff." He corked the bottle and pushed a glass across to Shorty. "Now what the hell d'we do?"

Shorty downed the whiskey in one gulp and pushed the glass back for a refill. "They got to be a way to open it."

"Yeh, there is. With the key."

Shorty watched the other fill the glass again. "But who the hell's got the key?"

Slater grunted. He drank the whiskey down, made a face, and poured another drink. "I been wonderin' about something."

"What?"

"Turk, he searched the body. What if he found a key?"

"You figger he'd hold out on us?" Shorty hadn't thought of that.

"He coulda found the key and not told us." Slater sipped the drink.

Shorty turned it over in his mind. "We get hold of the goddam box and we can't open it. But maybe Turk found the key when he searched."

"Then why'd Turk go to see Waco?"

"To throw us off. If he goes t'see Waco in Huffield don't that *prove* he ain't got the key?"

"Christ!" Slater was disgusted. It did add up, all right! If *he* had found the key he'd have kept silent about it—for a million dollars! Hell, he, Slater, would have done it for a hell of a lot less.

Shorty went on, warming to his idea. "So what's he do? He says to us, he says: 'Leave the box here in the cave and we'll come back for it later.'"

"That's right."

"What would he do if he had the key? What'd he do if he had the key and wanted to keep it all for hisself?"

"He'd say leave it here and we'll get it later." Slater pounded a fist into his hand. "Sonofabitch, Shorty! You got it right!"

"I bet you he's on his way to git it and hide it somewhere's else right now!"

Slater stared at the tall man. "Jesus!"

"Turk's goin' to double-cross us."

Slater gulped the rest of the drink. Jesus! Shorty was right! It was exactly what he himself would have done—tell the others it couldn't be opened, then go back for it later. He got up. "We got to go move that goddam box where he can't find it."

"Let's go. Hell, we don't need Turk no longer anyhow. We can get that goddam box open ourselves."

Turk Jessop rode into town that night late and went in the back way to Jake Higgins's Saloon. He and Jake were old friends; Jake was a good boy and owed him a favor or two. Jake came out to the back to greet him and Turk asked for a drink and the weekly.

"What you want the paper for, you in it?"

Turk laughed. "Hell, I ain't done a job for a year."

Jake didn't believe that, but he went back inside and returned with the newspaper. Turk sat down under a lantern and perused it.

The item was in the column all right, but it said the request had to go through Washington.

Jessup swore. He had half anticipated that. A two-bit clerk wouldn't have the power to give out that kind of money. He would have to wait it out, like it or not. Of course the steel box would keep. Nothing but dynamite would harm it, and they ought to have an answer next week.

"People looking for you," Jake told him. "The gossip is you wanted for murder and robbery."

70

"That so? Who'd I murder?"

"Feller named Atwood. Treasury agent." Jake pointed. "It's in the paper there."

Turk nodded. They didn't know about the one he'd shot and buried. He was one up on them. He said, "That's jus' newspaper talk, Jake. They don't know I shot nobody. I mean, they don't know it for damn sure."

"No witnesses, huh?"

"That's right. 'Less they got a witness, I didn't do it." He chuckled. "You-all mind if I use your storeroom cot tonight?"

"Hell no."

He spent the night in the storeroom and was up early to visit Rufe Wayda's store. Rufe was a locksmith, among other things, a tall, spare man with deep lines in his face and a mournful expression at the best of times.

Jessop told him about the box and the lack of a key.

"I heard about that box," Rufe said. "Gov'ment's not sayin' much, but the talk is, it got a million dollars in it."

"That's the talk, huh?"

"Izzat the box you got, Turk?"

"What if it is?"

Rufe made a face. "I figger you need it opened."

"Le's cut out the shit, Rufe. I got a steel box and no goddam key. Can you open it?"

"I got to see the box first. It sounds like hardened steel."

"Yeh. It got a funny kind of a lock on it. Never seen one like it before."

"Maybe I never either."

"Get your hat. We'll go look at it."

"How far is it?"

"'Bout a day's ride."

Rufe frowned. "Why can't you bring it in?"

"Too goddam heavy."

"You mean it's a safe!"

"Well, you could say that, I guess. Come on."

"I ain't got a horse."

71

"Well, go get one from the livery." Turk went to the door. "I'll meet you right north of the town."

"All right."

Turk turned to go, then came back. "And Rufe—keep your mouth shut."

Chapter Nine

THE funeral of John Atwood took place in the morning and was not elaborate. His parents, living in Pennsylvania, had been notified, but were unable, largely because of age, to make the long journey. He had been unmarried. His only brother was out of the country, no one knew exactly where.

The undertaker, Mr. Rasor, brought the casket to the cemetery in his black wagon with the glass sides and black lanterns on the four corners. As Reinhardt had specified, the body was in a plain pine box. Rasor had painted it dark brown, which modified its cheapness somewhat.

There were only four mourners: Reinhardt, Laredo and Pete Torres, and Bert Fortner. Gerard Quinlan had begged off, saying he was feeling ill.

A Methodist preacher, Mr. Harvey Strehl, had agreed to deliver a few appropriate words over the grave for five dollars. Mr. Strehl also took the opportunity to mention, as he concluded his eulogy, that he had a sorrel horse for sale that could be seen at the livery stable.

Reinhardt was very annoyed that Quinlan had not attended. "The sonofabitch got him killed and hasn't got the guts to come to the send-off. I wish to hell he was in that box instead of Johnny Atwood."

It was a weary, tiresome job, watching Maria Colosi's house. With her permission they made themselves at home in the stable, fixing the door ajar so they would be able to hear and see anyone coming along the alley. The stable also had several small windows; they could watch the rear house door through them.

But no one came near the house or stable except Maria. She went to the saloon each day about midday and returned late at night, usually coming home with one of the bartenders, who saw her safely to her door.

After two days of it Pete Torres said, "Maybe Jessop's got another girl."

It was a possibility.

Frank Slater and Shorty borrowed a stocky black mule and pack tree and went after the steel box. They hurried, afraid that Jessop had already moved it.

But he had not.

They were both astonished and delighted to find the shipment box exactly as they had left it. Jessop had taken his time, they said to each other, and they had gotten to it first. He was the one who was going to be surprised.

They heaved the heavy box up onto the pack tree and roped it securely, covering it with a square of canvas.

When Turk came for the box and found it had disappeared, he would of course know exactly who had taken it and he would come looking for them. For a million dollars they would take that chance. Turk had a reputation as a quick man with a gun, but they were two to his one, after all.

Taking a roundabout path, they brought the box back to Frank Slater's shack. It was probably the first place Turk would look for them, but Frank had an idea.

"If we shove this here box into the middle of that pile of cut wood out there, who'd think of looking for it?"

74

There was a large pile of cut logs and planks near the corn cribs, ready to be hauled into town next winter for Pete Cutler's fireplace. Slater had been chopping logs on and off all year.

Shorty agreed it was a marvelous idea.

"We leave it there a month or two, till all the hullabaloo dies down, then come and get it with a wagon and take it wherever we want."

"You sure it'll still be there?"

"Hell yes. Lissen, there's some brown paint in the barn. If we paint the box so's it don't give off a metal shine, no one will ever find it."

They dropped the box next to the wood. Slater opened the paint can and brushed a dirty brown paint over the dull metal, and when he was finished it looked very ordinary.

It took an hour to pile the wood over the box so it was completely hidden. Slater returned the paint can. Shorty took the mule and pack tree to the owner, then they made themselves scarce.

"Le's be smart for once," Slater said. "The law's lookin' for it, so is Turk, and none of 'em'll find it. When it all dies down and when we get good and ready we'll slip back some night and get it."

"Where we going till then?" Shorty asked.

Slater considered. "We could go to Frisco. . . ."

"Yeh. You got any money?"

"Not much."

"It costs money to go to Frisco. Got to stay in hotels. . . ."

"Lissen. I got a friend down south a ways, name of Dallas Laymon. He'n I usta ride wild over in Arizona. . . . We c'n go there and lay up till spring if we want."

Shorty nodded.

Rufe Wayda rented a nag at the livery and took the road north out of town. In the first mile he met Turk, and they left the road, heading northwest. Rufe had brought along a box of tools.

They reached the spot after dark and could not find the cave. They made a camp and looked again for it in the morning.

But the box was not where it had been left!

Turk was momentarily nonplussed. Could he have mistaken the spot? No—this was it, for sure. And now that he looked more carefully, there were fresh tracks on the earth. Someone had been here and lifted the box!

And it had to be Frank Slater and Shorty! It had to be! The chance of a stranger stumbling onto it was one in a trillion!

It was Slater and Shorty, all right. Jessop swore great oaths and stamped around in a rage—but no anger would make the box appear.

He got on his horse, thanked Rufe for his trouble, and lit out, leaving the locksmith to find his way back alone. He rode directly to Frank Slater's shack, reaching it near dusk. As he approached he drew his pistol. He would center Frank or Shorty as soon as he saw them!

But no one was home.

The interior of the house looked as if Slater had decamped. Jessop kicked things around in the shack, breaking down shelves and cutting the bed ropes in his spite. He completely destroyed the inside of the shack—and considered setting it afire. But he remembered that it was owned by someone else. . . .

Slater and Shorty had gone somewhere with the box. But where?

He went to see Carl Smith, the carpenter. But Smitty hadn't seen Shorty in a while, he said. "Two gents was here askin' about him. They looked like law."

That was to be expected. "You got any idee where Shorty would go to hole up?"

"He got cousins back east. . . . He never mentioned no kin around here."

"How about girls?"

Smitty shook his head. "Don't know."

When Jessop left Smitty's place he thought about Maria. Of course the law was sure to have the saloon covered. He might get into her house without being seen... but it was a chance. Should he take it or not? He sat on his horse and thought about it. He certainly did not want to be cornered in a house. . . .

Maria had told him in no uncertain words that she did not want to see him again in this life. He knew her to be a definite-minded woman. She probably meant it.

And she was capable of hiring a gunman to sit by her door, waiting. Maybe with a double-barreled shotgun . . .

Such a guard would have a tremendous advantage over someone trying to enter. Such thoughts greatly diluted his feelings about Maria.

There were other girls, after all.

He turned the horse and rode back into the hills. Forget Maria.

Where would he find Shorty and Frank Slater? That was the big question. Could they get far with the heavy steel box? It would be very damned visible, unless they put it on a wagon and covered it.

There was a railroad out of Carson City. Would they have the nerve to put the metal shipment box on a train? Every lawman in the country had probably been notified that it had been stolen. Such a box would be instantly suspect. They probably had not.

But there were several roads out of the city. Which one should he try first? Which direction would they go? He tried to put himself in Slater's position, think like him. It was foolish to try to think like Shorty; Shorty was not known for brains.

But Slater was not stupid. What would he do? Of course he would try to open the box. . . . He would probably try all the things Jessop had already tried. He'd try them in a different place—maybe Reno.

Jessop headed for that town.

* * *

Doyle Reinhardt received an official wire from Washington, instructing him to put Gerard Quinlan on a train to D.C. at once to appear before a board.

Bert Fortner was also instructed to board the train. His testimony was needed.

In the matter of the ransom, Reinhardt was informed that the government would not deal with thieves and murderers. Nothing would be offered for the return of the steel shipment box. But the criminals were warned that when they were caught, the full weight of the government would come down on them. They would be prosecuted to the limit. They could look forward to a great many years as guests of the people in a federal prison. Perhaps they would even hang.

Reinhardt duly inserted this paraphrased notice in the weekly paper, under the code name Rainbow.

Fritz Benner had given the matter of the shipment a good deal of thought. Erich Ganz had failed him in Chicago, but it was likely Ganz had acted foolishly or impetuously—his report had been vague. He would do without Ganz.

How many times in his life had he been close to several millions? Not often. Such a prize was worth a power of trouble. It would mean an end to all the hundreds of schemes and deals that took up his days now; the constant worry that some underling would inform on him; the everlasting covering of his tracks. . . .

He wrote several letters and bought a ticket for Chicago.

When he arrived the Trask brothers were waiting for him. They were toughs, experienced thugs, Pony and Homer. Homer was nicknamed Gumbo. Both men had worked for him many times and he had found them durable, close-mouthed, a little stupid, but able to follow orders. Benner was sure that with his brains and the Trasks' muscle, he would be able to get his hands on the shipment.

Then, off to Europe to let the hue and cry subside.

According to the latest information he'd been able to

glean from the newspapers, the million-dollar shipment box had not turned up, which undoubtedly meant that someone or some gang had stolen it. Such a box does not get lost in the trash.

He bought three tickets in Chicago and arrived in Carson City in due time.

At once he sent Pony and Gumbo out to ask questions. They would offer money around in likely places in exchange for information.

Offering money brought results.

Pony learned about Turk Jessop, and was shown the weekly's news stories. Jessop was described as a very hard case who usually got what he went after—one way or another. It was known that he had been after the missing shipment from the Treasury Department. Many thought he had it. He was no longer around in his usual haunts. If he had it, he had probably gone to the bright lights. . . .

Gumbo turned up Maria Colosi, and heard about Slater and Shorty.

Since Jessop's sidekicks, Slater and Shorty, were also no longer around, it was assumed in the saloons that Turk Jessop had gotten rid of them and had the loot for himself. It would be like him, everyone said.

Gumbo learned that Maria had once been Jessop's light o' life, but was no longer. Or perhaps it was the other way round. At any rate, they were on the outs.

Maria would not see him, would tell him nothing. Her bouncer escorted Gumbo to the sidewalk.

When they told it all to Benner, he thought the theory that Jessop had gotten rid of the two sidekicks was logical. It was the way he would have worked. . . .

"But where is this Jessop now?"

"Nobody's seen him," Gumbo said.

"Find him," Benner ordered. But as they went to the door he said, "Don't bring him to me dead. He's no goddam good dead—hear?"

"You want the box."

"Exactly. The box is the important thing."

They said they understood, and left—wondering where to begin.

Fritz Benner had thought the matter through, and decided to go all-out for the missing Treasury package. If it contained what what's-his-name, the government clerk, had told him in Washington in the carriage, he would never have a better opportunity to become very rich—rather quickly.

So he had come to the Far West in secret, prepared to do anything necessary to gain his ends. He was a believer in force.

Pony and Gumbo also believed in force. They had relied on it all their lives, and for the most part it had paid them well. Of course they had spent a few years behind bars . . . but that was part of the only life they knew.

They were a formidable pair and looked very much alike. Pony was the younger by a year, and possibly the quicker with his hands. They were both stocky and dark, with heavy jowls and deep-set eyes. In the East they had been partial to armed robbery or smash and grab.

They were not particularly tactful and made no attempts to cover their activities. As soon as they began passing around Fritz Benner's money, asking for information about Jessop, Slater, Shorty, and Maria, they were noticed by Doyle Reinhardt's sources—and duly reported.

Reinhardt informed Laredo and Pete Torres at once that certain toughs, new to the area, were in town asking about Jessop and presumably about the missing shipment.

The toughs were pointed out to them. It was child's play to tail them back to Fritz Benner. Benner, they quickly learned, had recently come to town from Washington, D.C.

Laredo wired John Fleming at once to say that Benner had come west, and asked for more information on him. How had Benner known about the shipment?

Fleming wired back that Benner was known as one who worked behind the scenes, paid for his dirty work, and kept well clear of it. It had been difficult to pin anything on him in the past. However, the investigation that had been initiated at the first mention of his name had been successful. They had turned up a man who had taken his superior's place for a short time and had sold information of the shipment to Benner. The man's name was Victor Kolby; he had confessed and was awaiting trial.

However, Kolby had nothing in writing; it was his word against Benner's. There were no witnesses; Benner had not been charged.

Turk Jessop arrived in Reno at noontime and immediately looked up several friends who kept their ears to the ground. Had either of them seen Frank Slater or Shorty?

"Not for months," both said.

"They haven't been seen in Reno lately?"

"No. Not unless they just passed through."

Jessop was deflated. He had been sure they'd come this way. If they had passed through, where would they be bound? He had no idea. He swore and kicked things, and finally took stock. They must have gone in the other direction, toward San Francisco. Shit!

There was nothing for it but to get on his horse and return. He had wasted days.

Frank Slater had been to Dallas Laymon's tar-paper shack once before, but it took most of a day to find it after they turned off the main road—which was only a two-track cart or wagon trail, heavily overgrown with weeds.

Dallas was glad to see them. He was a big, lanky man, good-natured and easygoing. "Happy as hell t'have the company," he said. "It's mighty goddam lonesome out here in the sticks all by m'self." He shook with both of them. "Nothin' but the stock to talk to, and the opinion of a cow ain't worth a damn."

"Good t'see you, Dallas," Frank said. "You ain't changed a hair."

"Come on in the house. I got a bottle. This here calls for a celebration." He paused. "You-all ain't one jump ahead of a sheriff, are you?"

"Not this time," Slater said. "Not wanted for a thing. Not by the law anyways. We had a little ruckus with some fellers and lit out—but that's another story." He and Shorty had decided on that story if Dallas got curious about their showing up suddenly.

Dallas didn't ask any questions, even though he was not convinced by the story. But the hell with the law. He had been in jail himself once or twice and didn't wish it on anyone. If Frank and Shorty were running from the law, this was a good place to lay up. The law probably couldn't find it.

They had a drink from the bottle and Frank made it clear he and Shorty would pay their way, so nothing more was said.

Dallas ran a few hundred cows and a dozen horses and got by. His house was well off the beaten track, fifty miles from the nearest town, so he only went in once or maybe twice a month for supplies, and maybe a little fun with the saloon girls.

The house was a big shack, tar paper and boards with a shingle roof that was curling in the sun. Dallas said he'd gotten close to a gal in town, but had never worked up the nerve to ask her to come out and live in it. The house was drafty and often the fireplace filled the room with smoke; the chimney didn't draw well.

After the second night, Shorty got up on the roof with a rope and a bundle of rags and worked at cleaning out the chimney. It helped.

Soon after that, to battle the boredom, Slater found a hammer and nails and went around fixing obvious holes and slits in the walls.

Dallas said it was like Christmas, having them there. He hoped they'd stay a long time.

Shorty seemed content; he helped Dallas with the stock.

But Slater was edgy after a week. What the hell was happening in the world? He talked about riding into town for a newspaper.

"I'm goin' in, in about a week," Dallas told him. "You c'n go with me."

Slater began riding far out on the range, anything to keep moving. He could not understand how a man could spend his life out in the sticks away from everyone. Dallas was an enigma to him. Jesus! When he got his hands on the money he would head for the big towns and kick up his heels, get drunk and chase girls—he was going to have some fun! He was going to live!

While Slater was gone, Shorty and Dallas talked. They got on famously, the same breed of cat. He and Frank were not wanted by the law, Shorty said over and over. They just needed a change. Nothing serious.

Dallas believed none of it, but never argued. They were a long way from the Carson City law anyway. Nothing they did down here would ever get back to Nevada.

Frank Slater helped him hook up the team the following week and they made the long drive into town.

It was a mining and cow town, big enough to have its own weekly newspaper, though mostly reprints from San Francisco. Slater bought a paper and sat in a saloon sipping beer, reading the news, listening to people jabber around him. This was what he'd been lacking, and he soaked it up.

Dallas left his grocery and supply list with the owner of the general store and went outside to smoke a cigar. Across the street was the newspaper office, with the name of the paper in gold leaf on the glass windows.

Dallas looked at it and puffed the cigar. He had never in his life seen his name in print. And as he stared, he thought of a way to do that. He walked across the street and talked to a young man with a green eyeshade. The young man took down the particulars in a neat, careful hand.

Two friends were staying with him for the time being,

Dallas said. They were from Carson City and were enjoying their sojourn. He did not mention Slater or Shorty by name.

And he didn't bother to tell Slater what he'd done. It wouldn't mean anything to him or Shorty.

Chapter Ten

Iᴛ was not difficult for a man to disappear from his usual haunts. All he had to do was get on a horse and ride in one direction or another, and keep riding. The desert or the mountains would swallow him up—and if he chose, his old surroundings would never see him again.

Turk Jessop, Slater, and Shorty could have done just that. Taking the shipment box with them.

Laredo and Pete Torres visited all the saloons and bawdy houses once frequented by the three, but no one had a thing to tell them. They kept their eyes on the two Trask brothers, but it was obvious from their movements that they were at loose ends also.

Then Doyle Reinhardt had a visitor from Reno who swore that Turk Jessop had been in that town very recently —alone. "He was askin' for Frank Slater and Shorty," the man said.

"Did he find them?"

"Hell no. Rode right outa town. Said somethin' about going to Frisco."

Reinhardt reported the conversation to Laredo and Pete.

"They split up all right. And it sounds like Jessop has lost the box. He's looking for it."

"Double cross?"

"That's my guess." Reinhardt nodded. "We've got a man in San Francisco. I'll wire him to keep his eye peeled for Jessop. If he shows up there, we can keep track of him."

Peter Cutler was tired. He had been a merchant in Carson City for eleven years, selling dry goods. His wife had died some years past and he was thinking ahead to getting out, retiring. He had always made a living and had put money by; enough, he thought, to last him his remaining years—he was fifty-two. He would have enough without working from sun-up to sunset, if he lived a fairly spartan life, probably in another town. He had long thought of going to San Francisco, where his younger sister lived. She wrote him that a body could live there more cheaply.

He would sell the store in town and probably get a good price for it. It contained a small apartment where the owner could live if he desired. His books would show a steady business. He thought about putting a notice in the paper.

He would also sell the bit of land he owned outside of town. He had four acres that he'd bought just before his wife died. He had thought to build a house on it; she had been behind that idea. But now that she was gone, he cared little about it. He hadn't even seen the land for a couple of years.

One Sunday, after church, he hooked up his buggy and drove out to look at the plot, wondering if he could get out of it what he'd paid. A few years ago a neighbor had built a row of corn cribs on the land, paying him a small rental.

There was also a tar paper shack that he allowed Frank Slater to use. Frank paid him back with chores. He didn't have a high opinion of Slater; the chores often didn't get done. Frank was full of excuses.

Cutler was surprised to find that Frank was not in the shack and had apparently not been in it for some time. In fact, the shack was nearly a ruin inside. Shelves were knocked down, the furniture smashed, bed ropes cut—it looked as if someone had deliberately wrecked it.

Cutler sighed, shaking his gray head. Probably Frank had gotten wild drunk and had smashed things up—then gotten out when he sobered up and saw what he'd done.

But at least Frank had done what he promised. There was a huge pile of cut wood ready for the stove. That was something. Cutler looked at the sky. Summer was here and winter would soon follow. He would wait till spring to put the store up for sale. He got in the buggy and drove back into town.

On Monday morning he called in Ernie Miller. Ernie was twenty-seven and strong as a young bull. Ernie's ability was strength, not brains, but he could follow simple orders.

Cutler said, "You ride out to my place—you know where it is?"

Ernie nodded his dark head. "Them four acres where Frank Slater lives?"

"Yes. You take the wagon and bring in that pile of cut wood, rick it up outside here. It'll prob'ly take you two, three trips."

"All right."

"Then you can clean out the shack. It's a damn mess in there. Frank's gone."

"He is?"

"Yes. Nowhere's around anyway. If he shows up, you tell him I want t'see him. Hear?"

"Yessir, Mr. Cutler." Ernie stomped out and pulled the wagon out of the stable. He hitched up the horse and drove out to the shack, humming to himself.

He halted the wagon by the wood, a hell of a big pile of it. This was going to take him all day. Pulling on a pair of leather gloves, he set about tossing the cut logs into the wagon.

About the middle of the afternoon he discovered the metal box. It was heavy as hell and was painted dark

87

brown. Ernie scratched his head, staring at it. What was a box like that doing in the middle of a pile of wood?

It was a chore, getting it into the wagon bed. It was heavy as a cow. He drove back into town and into the alley behind Cutler's store. Cutler was astonished to see the metal box.

"Where'd that come from?"

"It was buried in the pile of wood. Ain't it yours?"

Cutler cleared his throat. "Yes, of course it's mine. Bring it inside. We'll have a look at it."

Ernie struggled to get it in the door. He muscled it to a place in a corner that Cutler indicated. Then Cutler noticed the keyhole. This was a safe! He sent Ernie out to rick up the wood against the wall, and squatted down by the box. Jesus! Was this the metal box the Treasury had lost? There was gossip about it all over town.

Had Frank Slater stolen it and hidden it in the woodpile? Who else?

Someone had put a coat of brown paint on the box, maybe as camouflage. But this sure as hell was the Treasury box. He could make out a few of the black letters under the paint.

Gossip said it was worth more than a million dollars!

Peter Cutler licked his thin lips. A million dollars! And it had just fallen into his lap. No more worrying about the next month. No more worrying about making ends meet. . . .

It never once occurred to him to claim a reward.

He draped a piece of canvas over the box and told Ernie to say nothing about it. Ernie promised.

Cutler had seen at a glance that the box had no ordinary lock. He knew about locks from long experience as a merchant. He would have to find a locksmith who not only could unlock it but could keep his mouth shut afterward. That meant he would have to bribe someone heavily. Well, it would be worth it.

But he was sure that the town had no locksmith capable

88

of opening it. Rufe Wayda said he was a locksmith, but he was really only a handyman.

He pondered the matter. What if he put the box on a wagon and hauled it to a big town, Reno or San Francisco? It was a long way to Frisco. . . . But then he could hire a locksmith to open it, and get out of town the same day. He might even lose himself in a town as big as San Francisco. They wouldn't know who to look for. He would put whatever was in the box into a valise or two, then take the stage or a ship and get completely out of the country.

If there *was* a million in the box, he'd just forget about the store in Carson City. What was a couple of thousand?

Thinking about it made him feel very good. Several times that day he lifted the canvas to look and to feel the cold steel box.

Ernie finished with the wood and climbed on the wagon to go back out to the shack. Cutler watched him go. Ernie was not a terribly bright boy. Could he depend on Ernie to keep his mouth shut? He'd told Ernie the box was his; maybe the boy hadn't given it another thought.

Cutler went home that night, as usual, heated himself some soup, and ate it, tearing off chunks of bread absently. His thoughts returned constantly to Ernie. Could he really trust the boy to keep shut?

If he was so worried about it—probably not.

He paced the floor. A million dollars! Wasn't he foolish to put himself in Ernie's hands? If Ernie talked and the law got wind of it they'd come and take the box away from him, and might even put him in jail because he hadn't reported it. There was no telling what some damned sheriff might do.

He ought to go visit his sister in San Francisco. And he ought to leave tonight!

He hurriedly put some food in a sack, grabbed his coat, and ran out. He'd never get this close to that much money again in his life.

At the store he hitched up the wagon and backed it to the rear door. It took everything he had to get the heavy box up into the wagon bed, and when it was there he was exhausted. He covered it with the canvas, locked the store securely, and drove the wagon out of town.

He headed west, for Tahoe. He would take the road around the lake, over the hills into the great valley.

That evening Ernie Miller spent some of his wages in Jake Higgins's saloon. Ernie was a nondescript sort; he had an open, bland face and a stumbling way of speaking. No one had ever listened to him for more than a minute in his life. A person could look at Ernie and know he had nothing to say. Everyone ignored him. If he struck up a conversation with an absolute stranger, that person would, rather soon, move away and start talking to someone else.

Only once in a great while had Ernie been able to attract attention. Once he had burst into a saloon to yell that the livery stable was on fire! They listened to him then. He had cleared the room.

Another time there had been a shooting. A gambler had shot someone and had jumped on his horse and hightailed it out of town. Ernie had seen him go. When a couple of men, friends of the recently deceased, had mounted up to go after the killer, they had started the wrong way. Ernie had shouted at them and put them right.

So when he had something to say, people listened to him.

He wandered around the saloon, watching men play poker. He tried to talk to the girls, but they always slid away from him.

It was late when he remembered the metal box. Damn funny, finding that box in a woodpile. He went to the bar to tell Jake about it. But Jake nodded to him and moved away. He followed Jake down the bar. "I found a box today, Jake."

"Yeh, Kid, that's nice." Jake began talking to several men.

Ernie waited. After a long while Jake moved toward him, mopping the bar with a rag. Ernie said, "It was a big, metal box, painted brown."

90

"What?"

"I found this box today. Heavy as sin."

Jake stopped mopping. "What? You found what?"

"A big metal box in a woodpile."

A furrow gathered between Jake's thick brows. "A big metal box?"

Ernie nodded eagerly. He could see he had Jake's attention. "It was hidden in a pile of cut firewood." It pleased something inside him when Jake leaned over the bar and spoke directly to him in a whisper.

"Where was this, Ernie?"

"Over at old Cutler's place. You know, where Frank Slater lives in that shack."

"What'd you do with the box?"

"Took it to Cutler's store. He said it was his. Why'd he put it in a pile of firewood?"

"Is it in the store now?"

"Yeh, I guess so."

Jake nodded and reached out to squeeze Ernie's arm. "Don't tell this around, kid." He drew a beer and slid it in front of Ernie. "This's on the house."

"Thanks, Jake." Ernie was very pleased.

"Sure, kid." Jake went down the bar and tossed the rag aside. He said something to the other barman and went out the back, pulling off the apron.

He hurried to Smitty's house and pounded on the door. When Smitty opened it, Jake slipped inside and shut the door behind him. Smitty was barefoot, in a shirt and pants, the shirttails hanging out.

"I was just goin' to bed. What's up? You got troubles?"

"No trouble. Get your boots on. You got a wagon?"

"Course I got a wagon. What the hell's up?"

Jake was excited. The words tumbled out. "I know where the Treasury shipment box is!"

"Christ!" Smitty stared at him. "Ever'body lookin' all over hell for that!"

"Well, they don't know their ass. They lookin' in the

wrong places. C'mon, get your boots on!" He followed Smitty into the bedroom.

"Where is it?" Smitty sat and pulled on a boot.

"Over at Cutler's store."

"For crissakes! You sayin' that Pete Cutler's got it?"

"Yeh. Come on, let's go!"

Smitty stomped on the boots, grabbed a coat, shoved a pistol into his waistband, and led the way out the back door to the stable. He had a light buckboard. Jake pulled it out from under the eaves as Smitty backed a gray horse into the shafts and hooked up.

They drove to the alley behind the Cutler store and halted. The row of stores was dark. Jake jumped down. The rear door to Cutler's store was locked, a big padlock through a hasp. Smitty looked at it and went back to the wagon, pulled out a crowbar, and levered the hasp out of the dry wood in a moment. It made a loud ripping sound; Jake peered around but there was no one near.

Smitty opened the door and went inside, striking a match. He found a candle stuck in a bottleneck and lit it. There was no metal box in the back of the store. Jake took the candle into the front. There was no box there either. He swore.

Smitty growled. "I thought you said it was here."

"Goddammit! That shitty little Ernie Miller told me it was! Said he brought it here to the store from his place outside town."

Smitty frowned at the clutter in the back room. "Somebody's sure as hell scrabbled around in here. Maybe Cutler took the box somewheres else."

"Took it where?"

Smitty shrugged. "Well, don't it look like somebody went through this place? Where does Cutler live?"

"That's an idee. He lives in that row of houses back of Maria's saloon."

"Is he married?"

"His wife died awhile back. Come on." Jake blew out the candle and they hurried out to the wagon. Smitty slapped the reins and they drove to the row of dark houses. Cutler's name was on a mailbox but the house was dark.

Smitty said, "He's in bed."

Jake jumped down and ran to the door to pound on it. No one answered.

Smitty came up behind him. "Maybe he ain't home."

Jake pounded again, harder. "He gotta be home!"

Smitty looked up at the windows. "Cutler knows what's in the box, Jake. He taken off. What you think?"

Jake blew out his breath and sagged against the door. "Yeah . . ." He looked at the other. "Where would he go?"

"Where would you go, you had a lot of money to spend?"

"New Orleans."

Smitty nodded. "One of them places."

One of Reinhardt's "sources," a skinny, no-account drifter named Calley, met him at the door to his house. It was a dark night, with a layer of fog settling lower in the street.

Reinhardt pulled a pistol, seeing the shadow move toward him. Calley said, "It's me, Mr. Reinhardt, Calley."

Reinhardt put his key in the lock and motioned Calley inside. He struck a match in the hall and lit a lantern where there were no windows. Calley was edgy about being seen.

"What is it, Calley?"

"I got something. Maybe it's good. . . ."

"All right. You want a drink of something?"

"Yeh. I could use it, Mist' Reinhardt."

Reinhardt went into the parlor and returned with a bottle and two glasses. He pulled the cork and poured into them. Calley downed his in a gulp. Reinhardt poured more.

"What you got for me?"

"I was at Jake's place. You know, Jake Higgins."

Reinhardt nodded.

"A feller named Ernie something came in and hung around. Then I seen him talking to Jake. In a minute Jake gives him a beer on the house, and Jake goes out the back. He didn't come back in."

"You hear what they said?"

Calley shook his head and gulped more whiskey. "But after Jake left Ernie was talking to some others, said he found a box."

"What about a box?"

"Said it belonged to old Pete Cutler."

"The dry goods store?"

"Yeh. Well, nobody wanted t'listen to Ernie, but I asked him how he found it and he told me it was in a pile of firewood."

"A pile of firewood?"

"Yeh. That's what he said. It was on Cutler's place outside town where Frank Slater lived."

Reinhardt smiled.

"That's it, Mr. Reinhardt. Is it anything?"

"You did good, Calley." Reinhardt gave him five dollars and saw him out.

So Frank Slater had had the box! He had hidden it in a pile of wood and Pete Cutler had stumbled onto it!

Reinhardt pulled on a coat and hurried to the hotel to talk to Laredo and Pete.

Chapter Eleven

"**F**RANK Slater was living in the shack on Cutler's property," Reinhardt told Laredo and Pete. "He must have put the box in the woodpile figuring to come back for it later."

"Where does Cutler live?" Laredo pulled on a coat. "We've got to talk to him."

"I'll show you."

It was nearly two in the morning when they arrived at Cutler's house. It was dark and no one answered the door. After a few minutes' rapping, a neighbor opened his door and called to them, "He isn't home."

Laredo walked across to the neighbor's door. "Do you know where he went?"

"I haven't seen him. What's all the excitement? Some others were here earlier looking for him."

"We have to talk to him," Laredo said. "Sorry for the noise." He went back to the others. "Let's go to his store."

But the store was dark too, and when they went around to the back, they found the lock had been broken. Someone had forced his way inside. There was evidence of a hasty departure.

"Cutler has flown with the shipment box," Reinhardt said heavily.

"It looks that way."

Pete said, "He's gone because he knows what's inside the box. He'd go where he thought he could get the box open, of course."

"That's right," Reinhardt agreed. "If he didn't know, he wouldn't have run. That makes him a thief."

"So he's headed for a large town, maybe Reno, maybe even San Francisco. How many ways to get to San Francisco?"

"Half a dozen," Reinhardt said with a sigh. "And he's got a big head start."

"That might be a dangerous journey for a man with a million-dollar steel box," Pete observed.

"He'll have to haul it in a wagon. . . ."

"And camouflage it with something. . . . But that should be easy," Laredo said. He looked at Pete. "What's your vote? Do we head for San Francisco?"

"I think it's our best bet."

Laredo nodded. "The neighbor said someone else had been knocking on the door earlier tonight. Maybe someone else knows Cutler has the box."

"If so they're probably on the road, chasing him right now."

Pete said, "This Ernie must have a big mouth."

"Big enough," Reinhardt said, grunting.

Laredo and Pete started out at sun-up, traveling light. The weather was chilly, gradually cooling, but it did not rain to muddy the road. They rode toward Tahoe and quickly discovered that two other men had also been inquiring along the way about a man driving a wagon.

Pete asked, "Did Slater come back for the box and find it missing? Is he on the road ahead of us?"

"If he did, why would he think Cutler had it?"

"Maybe he heard the same gossip—maybe Reinhardt's

96

source sold the information to someone else."

Laredo said, "You have a suspicious mind."

"I'm a highly trained detective. What if it's not Slater and Shorty ahead of us?"

"How many could be after the damned box?"

"Half the town. A million dollars doesn't grow on bushes." Laredo agreed. "At least not around here."

Fritz Benner was a man who kept up on the news. It sometimes paid off for him, so he read the newspapers front to back, filing away in his mind interesting bits of information. A man could not have too much information. He stored it away like canned goods on a shelf.

He read every newspaper he got his hands on. Over the years it had become habit—perhaps hobby. He taught himself to scan, to pass quickly by items he had already read about in other papers. He could scan the average weekly in minutes.

He tipped the hotel clerk to bring him out-of-town papers also. In one there was a column of folksy items, even home recipes and remedies. . . . Benner skipped such items as a rule. When he finished the paper he put it aside, on the stack by the door.

It was the last paper he'd received from the clerk. When he'd read it he lit a cigar and went to the window, staring out. Something was vaguely nagging at him. Had he forgotten something? He went to his desk and looked at notes. No, nothing like that. But something was bothering him. What the hell was it?

Was it something in the paper he'd just read?

He picked it off the stack and sat down to peruse it again, page by page, column by column, methodically. When he glanced down the column of homely items, two words seemed to stand out: Carson City.

Two men from Carson City were visiting someone called Dallas Laymon, on his ranch. Could they be Frank Slater and Shorty? With his box?

Of course they could be!

He put on his coat, went downstairs, and had the desk clerk send a boy for Pony and Gumbo.

It was an hour before they arrived and Benner was pacing the floor. He showed them the item.

"You take this paper and go to the office and find out where this Dallas Laymon lives. Tell 'em you're cousins or something. Then you go to the ranch."

"You want us t'bring both of them back?"

"Just one'll do. Bring back Slater. You know what he looks like?"

They both nodded.

Pony said, "I thought you wanted the box."

"That's right. The box is the important thing. I don't give a damn about anything else. If you find out where the box is, forget about them."

"All right." They hurried out, and were on their way inside an hour.

The newspaper Benner had given them was *The Fort Kane Telegraph*, serving Denton County. They were several days on the journey and found Fort Kane to be a mining and cow town, bustling with its own importance. It was on a stageline, was a freight depot, and there were rumors of a railroad spur line being built into town the following year.

They stopped off at the nearest saloon and had a drink. They had discussed the box for days. Gossip said it had a million dollars in it. Gumbo was all for finding the box and buying a ticket for South America. Pony was sure Benner would find them, no matter where they went.

Gumbo was willing to take the chance.

But first, they had to find the box. Gumbo took the newspaper and went across the street into the *Telegraph* office and asked to see someone who could tell him about the circled item. He was taken to a man with buck teeth and thick spectacles.

"What d'you want to know?"

Gumbo managed a smile. "I want t'go visit Dallas. He's an old friend. But I never been to his place. You got any idee how I get there?"

"Oh, izzat all. . . . Well, the ranch is about fifty miles west and south. Take the road out of town that goes past Hedgerson's Grain and Feed store. It's a big barn, you can't miss it." The man rubbed his jaw. "The trouble's going to be the cutoff road. I doubt if it's marked. It's about forty miles out—goes off to the south."

"Do you know if Dallas got any hands workin' for him?"

"I don't think so. He's scratching for a living."

"Thanks."

"Sure. You keep your eye peeled for that cutoff road now. . . ."

"I will."

The two stayed in town that night and set out in the morning. It would take all day and even part of the next, if the land was hard. The road was not much, a weedy two-track leading southwest from the town, not well traveled. It took the easiest course, around hills, across washes, and they met no one at all. Several dim tracks led off to the right, but not one to the left as the newspaper man had said. By nightfall they had not seen any cutoff road.

They camped off the road, listening to coyotes howl as they sat by a tiny fire. Gumbo said they were fools to take the box back to Benner when they could have it all. "There ain't nothing we couldn't do with a million dollars."

"Benner would have us hunted down."

"He'd have to find us. . . ." They settled nothing.

In the morning they found a path five miles farther on. It snaked off to the south and looked as if a wagon might have passed that way months ago. They agreed this must be the road.

It was the middle of the afternoon before they came in sight of a roofline. They halted instantly and got down, picketing the horses in thick brush. "That's got to be it," Pony said.

"We'd best wait and go in after dark."

"What if there's dogs?"

Gumbo slid a bowie knife from his belt. "They got to take their chances."

They came across a ravine that seemed to wander past the distant house, and followed it. From it, peering through brush, they could see several men at the house. There was also a barn and some corrals. It was too far to recognize anyone.

It took forever for the sun to go down; when it was full dark they approached the house and met no dogs. The house had no blinds or curtains and they could easily see in. One of the men inside was well over six feet—Shorty.

They had the right place.

But there were three of them, all well armed. They would be smart to think about what they were going to do, Pony said. It might not be a good idea to go up against three. Maybe they could whittle the numbers down. . . .

They went back to the horses and moved several miles to spend the night. Gumbo made a small fire in a hollow and they talked. Maybe they could pick off one or two of them from a distance, to even the odds. . . .

But if they started shooting Shorty or Slater would probably slip away. It would be impossible for only two men to watch all directions. It was a problem.

They had not settled it in the morning when they crawled close to the old shack to watch, and were surprised to see two men hitching up a buckboard. One was Slater and the other must be Dallas. The two got in the wagon, with Dallas driving and Slater levering a Winchester.

Pony swore, seeing them head for town, but Gumbo said, "We oughta be able to hog-tie Shorty and sweat it outa him. Them two'll be gone for days."

When the wagon was well out of sight, they began to move toward the house. But Shorty appeared suddenly from the barn, mounted on a sorrel horse, and galloped away to the south.

They had to swear and watch him go. He would spot them quickly if they tried to follow. There was nothing they could do but catch him coming back. They took up positions near the south trail and waited.

But Shorty evaded them again. He returned to the barn from the west, put the horse in a stall, and walked to the house before they realized he had returned.

There was too damned much country to watch, Pony growled. As it got dark Shorty lit several lanterns, and now and then they could see him passing a window. . . .

When it was full dark Gumbo said, "Now let's move in and get him. We'll throw down on him and tie 'im up—all right?"

"Yeh," Pony said.

They moved in close to the house, sure that Shorty could not see into the dark. But they were clumsy. Dallas Laymon was not a neat and tidy man. Who the hell would see it if he chopped firewood and let it scatter and pile up any old way in front of the house? When he wanted a stick all he had to do was reach down off the porch.

Pony stumbled over several sticks—and inside the house Shorty stiffened. He stepped to the closest lamp instantly and blew it out. Then he slid into the next room and blew that one out too. The house was darker than outside.

Shorty drew his revolver. Someone was out there, and it wasn't a coyote. Could it be an Indian? There were still some around—but would an Indian stumble over firewood? Shorty crouched down, waiting. Would he, or they, come in the door? Probably not.

They couldn't be lawmen, because by this time a deputy would have announced himself and invited him out.

Could it be somebody after the box? Could it be Jessop?

Jessop was the best bet, Shorty thought. But how in hell had Jessop tracked them here? That was a mystery. Maybe he had second sight.

Shorty considered. Frank Slater and Dallas wouldn't be back for another day and night at least. He was on his own. He had to slip out of the house; he could be trapped in it.

There wasn't a sound from outside. They knew he'd heard something because he'd blown out the lights. They knew he was wary and listening. Had he really heard what he thought he'd heard?

He couldn't take the chance that he hadn't.

It was only a three-room shack, not very large. Had Turk brought someone with him?... Did he have the house surrounded? There were two doors and half a dozen windows, none of which had glass. It was a fairly warm night, and they were all wide open now. Probably in the winter Dallas boarded them up.

Shorty moved to the back of the house and the floor creaked. He hadn't paid any attention to it before. Now the sound brought a shot. A bullet came in a window and slammed against the opposite wall, several feet from him. Too damned close!

Taking a long breath, Shorty sat on the floor and removed his boots.

A shadow crossed the window before him and he fired at it, rolling sideways at once. His shot brought two. Both smashed the chair near him, showering him with splinters.

He got up silently and slipped into the bedroom, intending to go through the window. If he could get outside he could probably lose them in the dark. He was sure he knew the lay of things better than they. If he could make one of the ravines nearby, they'd never catch him.

As he approached one of the windows, a shot blasted close by and he ducked away, seeing flashes of light suddenly. He had almost looked into the muzzle of a gun!

He retreated, momentarily blinded. More shots searched for him as he dropped to the floor. They smashed into the walls and one hit a lantern, shattering it to bits. Shorty crawled into the next room, breathing hard.

There were at least two of them!

This was a tight spot! He blinked, letting his eyes come slowly back to normal. What the hell was he going to do? He had to get out of the house before morning... because then they'd come in after him.

He sat up, wondering about his chances of getting out the front door.

Then he smelled smoke!

He got up, sniffing. It *was* smoke! He slid into the next

room and heard the unmistakable crackle of flames. They had set the house afire!

It was Pony's idea. "If we set the house on fire he'll have to come out."

"Won't he come out shooting?"

"Naw. We'll yell, tell him he's safe if he comes out peaceable." Pony reloaded his pistol. "We'll tell 'im we don't wanna shoot him, we wanna talk."

Gumbo nodded, thinking it over. The *hombre* would have to come out. . . . Pony was right about that. "All right. Let's set it in two places. I'll go around the back."

Gumbo gathered up dry sticks from the front, a good handful would do, and carried them around to the back of the shack. He made a little pile of them against the wall, very carefully. The shack was dry as dust. It would burn like a rocket.

Striking a match, he held it under the kindling, watching the orange flame grow. Smoke curled up, then the fire suddenly blazed, the flames reaching up. In minutes it was licking up the side of the house greedily. Gumbo backed away, grimacing. It was hot as hell!

He heard Pony yelling out front, telling the man inside he was safe if he came out.

His yell was answered by a fusillade; Shorty had emptied his pistol at the sound.

Pony shouted, "Don't be a damn fool! Come on out. We just wanna talk!"

There were more shots from inside. Shorty didn't believe them.

Gumbo ran around to the front. He yelled at his brother, "We got to get him out!"

Pony shook his head and pointed to the house. It was ablaze from two sides. It would be suicide to go in. All around the house it was bright as day. Gumbo shielded his eyes as shots came from inside—and Pony slumped suddenly.

Gumbo yelped and grabbed Pony, dragging him away

from the house. Thirty feet away he halted and felt for a pulse.

There was none.

He sat down abruptly. Pony dead? He stared at the inert body . . . then at the house. Fire poured out of the windows, licking at the tar-paper roof. Sparks shot a hundred feet into the air. The house was a torch! It seemed only minutes since they'd set it.

More shots sounded from within—then only the crackle of flames could be heard as the house was dissolved in fire.

"The sonofabitch's cooked," Gumbo said aloud.

He rolled Pony's body over. The shot had hit him in the ticker, dead center. Gumbo shook his head helplessly. Somehow he'd never thought death would grab one of them. . . . What was he going to do now?

Sighing deeply, he watched the house crumble and fall in on itself as sparks showered and flames danced. Once more a flurry of shots sounded, probably a box of ammo going up.

Well, Shorty was gone now. He'd never tell where the box was. And Frank Slater was the only one left. Shorty must have been dumb or crazy to stay in the house. . . .

What was he going to do now?

Well, the first thing was to bury Pony. He couldn't leave the body lying there. He got up and walked to the barn, feeling twenty years older. He found a blanket draped over a stall, and a shovel leaning against a wall. He went back, pulled off Pony's gunbelt and pistol, searched the body to pocket bills and coins, then wrapped it in the blanket.

Then he tramped back to bring the horses to the barn and sat with his back to the wall, watching the flames die down and smoulder. He was awake all night.

In the pale light of morning he dug a deep hole not far from the ruins of the house and buried Pony.

That done, he got on his horse, led the other, and headed south. To hell with Benner. Let the sonofabitch fight his own battles.

A mile away he looked back once.

Chapter Twelve

GERARD Quinlan was met at the station by Tom Quincy
and taken to a cheap hotel. Quincy had a letter, which he
passed over. It was from the commission appointed by the
Treasury Secretary, and required Gerard Quinlan to appear
before them in three days.

Bert Fortner had been taken to another hotel—apparently they were to be kept apart until the hearing. It was an
unnecessary move; they had not spoken five words to each
other on the long train trip across the continent.

The commission was composed of five men from the
Treasury Department, high officials whose job it was to
determine if there was any cause for criminal prosecution.
They were free to handle the matter in any way they
thought proper. None of them were lawyers.

They called Bert Fortner first. He sat in a chair facing
the five grim visages and related what had happened when
he, Quinlan, and John Atwood had been ambushed. "The
shots came from directly ahead and Atwood was hit immediately. I saw him fall, and Quinlan and I jumped from the
wagon into the brush. The wagon overturned in a ditch. We

were able to get into the ditch ourselves, otherwise we would have been killed too."

"Did you make any attempt to recover the shipment box?"

"No sir. There was no possibility of getting to it."

"But you did not try?"

"Three men were firing at us constantly, sir. The box was about twenty feet away. It would have been suicide to try to reach it."

"Did you prevent Mr. Quinlan from reaching it?"

Fortner hesitated. "I told him it was impossible, sir."

"But he wanted to try?"

Fortner shrugged. "I—I don't remember what he said, sir. We were under a terrible fire."

"I see. That will be all, Mr. Fortner."

Fortner started to rise. "May I say something, sir?"

"What?"

"In my opinion it was folly to have tried to take the shipment box to Reno. We should have put it on the train in Carson City."

"Is that all?"

"Yes sir."

"You are excused, Mr. Fortner."

Fortner got up and went out, closing the door.

Quinlan was called.

He went into the hearing room and sat in the chair. He acknowledged his name and was asked to tell his version of the ambush.

"Sir, the shots came unexpectedly. We were in the woods and visibility was poor. Mr. Atwood was hit very quickly, with the first shots. He had been driving the wagon and it overturned immediately when the mule bolted. Bert Fortner and I were able to jump out. I yelled at him to get into the ravine, which we both did. The shots continued, but it was impossible for us to tell where they came from."

"Did you make any attempt to recover the shipment box?"

"I told Bert—I mean Mr. Fortner—that we should use the overturned wagon as cover and creep close. I thought we would be very close to it then."

"What did Fortner say?"

"He did not want us to try, saying we would be killed."

"Did he restrain you in any way?"

Quinlan sighed. "Yes sir, I'm afraid so. He fought me when I attempted to crawl to the wagon, pulling me back. Please understand that we were in a very restricted space. If we rose up only an inch or two, we could be hit. The firing was continuous."

"Go on, Mr. Quinlan."

"Well, it was an impossible fight. I finally had to give in. He was stronger than I."

"I see. So then what happened?"

"We crawled along the ravine and finally got into the trees and got away from them. They were killers, sir."

"What about your decision to take the box to Reno?"

"I thought it best, sir. My only desire was to safeguard the shipment. Mr. Howard Wehr had been kidnapped—or at any rate had disappeared—so I was sure there was a plan afoot to get the box. We took every precaution to keep the movement secret."

"Is there anything you wish to say to us about Mr. Fortner's actions during that time?"

Quinlan paused. "I would rather not criticize him, sir. I believe he did what he thought at the time was right. There was a great deal of excitement you know, sir. If he lost his head it was only for a short time."

"I see. Thank you, Mr. Quinlan. That will be all."

Fritz Benner had had misgivings about the Trask brothers the moment they had left him. There was so much at stake; could he leave it to them alone? They were both excellent strong-arm lads, but they were not the smartest.

He had best go himself.

He put the word out, and interviewed several men who were recommended to him by one of the bartenders at the next-door saloon. They all looked like thugs but he finally selected one, Abner Parker, who seemed smart enough to come in out of the rain. Parker was big and rough-looking, but he was soft-spoken, which impressed Benner. He had a flattened nose and a deep scar on his forehead which he said he'd gotten during a boating accident.

Abner had a roan horse. Benner bought an animal from the livery and they set out for Fort Kane. No stage went directly to it from Carson City.

They arrived without event and got rooms in a hotel to rest and bathe. Benner sent Abner out to ask questions, but he learned nothing at all of Pony or Gumbo, until Benner suggested he try the newspaper.

A clerk at the weekly remembered a man asking about Dallas Laymon's ranch. "Said he was a friend, if I recall it right."

"What'd he want?"

"Directions to the ranch."

From the description the clerk gave, the questioner had been either Pony or his brother. Abner also received directions.

Benner was pleased. Maybe when they got to the ranch the brothers would have the box. They set out at once on the road the clerk indicated.

Doyle Reinhardt received a long coded wire from his superiors stating bald facts: Gerard Quinlan had been reinstated with a commendation. A hearing had found him blameless in the matter of the shipment box loss. He would return to Carson City very soon and take charge of the case again.

Bert Fortner's request for transfer had been granted. He would not return.

Reinhardt sat down abruptly, staring at the rectangle of paper. How could Washington be so stupid? Didn't they read reports? How could a hearing exonerate him when proper witnesses had not been asked to return and give testimony? Apparently the hearing commission had believed Quinlan and not Fortner.

Presumably it also meant that Quinlan had friends more powerful than anyone had suspected. The murder of John Atwood had been swept under the rug.

His own report on the matter had obviously been totally ignored.

"Makes you wonder about government," he said aloud.

Bert Fortner, a veteran in the department, had been reassigned. Bert would probably resign, Reinhardt thought. Now he'd have a black mark on his record. Quinlan had undoubtedly lied to the commission.

Reinhardt sighed. To all intents and purposes the case was going nowhere. It was practically closed. Laredo and Pete had gone after Cutler—but they could not be positive they were on the right track. Cutler might have taken another road or, when Laredo and Pete caught up with him. he might be totally innocent. Might not have the box at all.

That was not very likely, Reinhardt mused. But it *was* possible.

The department did not want to share the news of the robbery; the official line was silence. He, Reinhardt, could not ask for help from the citizenry. He was not sure that was the right course. His superiors said: "What would happen if we told everybody the box contains a million or more dollars? We'd never see it again."

Maybe. But there were honest men out there.

Well, it wasn't likely someone would be able to open the box. It would require very sophisticated tools and he doubted if there were very many west of the Mississippi. Maybe that was their only hope, that no one would be able to open the damned box! It was sure to turn up.

Of course, the sober thought interjected itself—there were always men who could do the unexpected.

Abner Parker and Fritz Benner were not plainsmen, nor were they trackers. They followed the dim trail that was

109

called a road for what they thought was forty miles, without seeing a road that turned off to the left.

Abner said, "I think we's lost, Mr. Benner."

"We're on the goddam road! How can we be lost?"

"Well, we haven't found the other road." He looked at the sky. "And it'll be dark in a few minutes."

They were forced to make camp by the road, and in the morning they retraced their steps in case they had missed the road to Laymon's ranch.

Benner was not positive what he would do when he confronted Shorty and Frank Slater; maybe he could work something out with them, and maybe he'd have to resort to violence. Abner could handle one of them, he'd take on the other. If they did it suddenly, it should be no contest.

But before they killed anyone, they'd have to know where the elusive box was. Slater and Shorty probably had it with them. That was the reason they were out here in the sticks. They were waiting for the fuss to die down. That was smart.

They had gone about a mile, retracing steps, when Abner noticed the dust cloud. He pointed it out. "Probably a wagon, comin' along this here road."

Benner reined in and leaned on the pommel. Maybe they could ask directions, but then—if he and Abner went to Laymon's ranch and had to kill someone—the man they asked directions of could describe them and point them out if it ever came to that.

Benner hated to put himself in another man's hands. He said, "Let's get off the road and let them go on by."

Abner shrugged and did not argue. They rode into the brush and halted to wait.

A half hour went by and no wagon appeared.

Abner said, "Maybe they stopped."

It was curious. Benner motioned. "Ride on down there, see if you can spot it."

Abner nodded and nudged the horse. He rode down the weedy road for about a mile and encountered no one. When he turned to come back he noticed the faint trails,

110

wheel marks, that turned off to the south. No wonder they hadn't seen the wagon; it had turned off.

He went back and told Benner.

In the wagon, Frank Slater and Dallas made good time. They had left the town while it was still dark, several hours before dawn, so that they'd get to the ranch by dark—with a little luck.

Twelve hours later they were approaching the house— except that no house was visible. At dusk they came in sight of the barn—where was the house?

They smelled ashes in another moment, and as they rode into the yard were stunned to find the house burned to the ground!

Dallas groaned. "What the hell happened?" He got down and walked around the blackened pyre. He glanced at Slater. "Where's Shorty?"

His horse was still in the barn, but he was nowhere about. Dallas yelled and fired his pistol, but no one answered.

Frank Slater was staring at the ruins of the house. "He's in there. Come over here—you can smell the burned flesh."

"Jesus! They burned him alive? If he was sleepin' the fire woulda woke him, wouldn't it?"

Slater was thinking of Jessop. "Maybe he couldn't get out. Maybe Turk Jessop was shootin' at him." Frank explained that he and Shorty had differences with Jessop and had come away to let the other cool off. "But he could have followed us here. I dunno how—but who else?"

"He wanted you dead?"

Slater made a face. "We never figgered that—but he's a mean bastard."

"Will he come back, lookin' for you?"

"He might. . . ." Slater got a rake and pulled at the ashes. He quickly came onto the body, blackened and shriveled. "Get a shovel, let's bury him. . . ."

* * *

That night they camped along a cliff line above a dry wash. If someone was looking for Slater, no one would find them there, Dallas promised. There were several boxes of supplies in the wagon, so they ate well and boiled coffee. After supper Dallas said he'd made up his mind.

"I'll go back into town. I can get me a carpenter to come out and whack up a place to live in for the time being. . . ."

"Damn me—I wish I had some money, Dallas. I feel bad about that house bein' burned."

"Hell, that old shack was half fallin' down anyways. I wouldn't even stay here, but I got them cows. Couple months I'll drive 'em to market and sell the whole she-bang."

Slater nodded. "Think I'll drift on south, too. Maybe get me a cowhand job."

They curled up in blankets and Slater lay awake for several hours. How in hell had Jessop managed to burn Shorty up? Maybe a lucky shot had centered him. That must have been it. Shorty had been dead or hit bad and the fire had got him. Too bad.

It was dark by the time Abner showed the wheel marks to Benner. Not a hell of a lot they could do, ramming around in the dark, Abner said. They'd be smart to camp till morning. Benner agreed.

In the morning they rode on, following the fresh wagon wheel trail, and came to the barn. Nearby a house had burned to the ground. There was no one around, and the barn was empty. The wagon was gone too.

Benner walked around, kicking things. It was a dead end. No Slater and no Shorty. Abner walked around looking for tracks, but the ground was hard and he found nothing he could recognize. He had never tracked anything in his life, but he did not tell that to Benner. Benner was boiling.

"Climb up on that goddam barn, see if you can see anything."

Abner followed orders. It was an easy climb, but as he sat on the ridgepole, staring around the horizon, he saw nothing moving. A hawk, high in the pale sky, studied him, but there was no other life in view. He climbed down slowly.

"What you wanta do next, Mr. Benner?"

Benner swore. He kicked a half-burned board into the pile of black ashes. "Let's get back into town."

Chapter Thirteen

Pᴇᴛᴇ Cutler was a worried man. He drove the gray horse all night and most of the next day with only short rests. He ate what food he had with him as the horse plodded along over the mountains, heading for the great valley.

He pulled off the road to sleep when he nearly fell from the wagon on a sharp turn. He hated to stop, but he had to have rest. He found a glade hidden from the road, tied the horse in a patch of grass, and curled up in the wagon bed next to the precious box. When he woke it was still dark, but his watch told him it must be close to dawn. He hooked up and got back on the road, to drive all day and half the next night.

He had plenty of time to think. He had been sure Ernie Miller would keep his mouth shut, but then Ernie was not the brightest. If the boy said anything out of the way, someone could pull the story out of him with little trouble. He knew that Ernie liked beer, and beer certainly loosened tongues.

If Ernie happened to mention finding a metal box, that would cause a curious question—certainly. And when the questioner learned the box had been hidden in a wood-pile! Well, that was so unusual that it would lead to many questions. . . . Someone would remember the Treasury shipment box, and two and two would be quickly put together.

Then they would drag his name out of Ernie. Then if someone went to the store and found it locked during a business day—that too would add to the suspicion.

And they would not be able to find him, Pete Cutler.

Cutler sighed. All in all he had probably left a pretty plain trail, hadn't he? Well, he had best assume he had, for safety's sake.

Turning, he gazed fondly at the tarpaulin-wrapped metal box. A million dollars was a powerful magnet. Men would kill for it in an instant. That idea caused an icicle to press against his spine. He was beginning to realize he was in terrible danger.

When he came to a fork in the road, he turned left because it seemed the lesser path. He had best stay off the main road.

In several hours he came to a little burg astraddle the road. It seemed fast asleep, no one about. His watch told him it was just past midnight. He pulled the wagon around behind a hay and feed store and halted by a corral. Taking the bit from the horse's mouth, he brought the animal a pail of water from a trough. Then he curled up in the wagon bed again.

The morning sun woke him; he was still woozy and half-asleep when the store owner unlocked the store. Cutler offered to pay for the space, but the owner said he was glad to help a pilgrim, although he accepted two bits for oats in a feed bag.

Cutler went across the street for breakfast in a steamy little restaurant and had the cook put up some food for the journey. He rolled out after eating and took the road southwest. No one seemed at all curious about what was in the wagon.

As he sat on the wagon seat watching the scenery slide

by, he thought more about leaving a trail. He had just left a good one. Probably everyone in the little burg could describe him. He ought to do something toward changing his appearance. What could he do?

The first thing he thought of was different clothes. He was wearing what everyone wore, pants, shirt, and coat. None of them new. If he bought new clothes everyone would stare at him. He did not ever remember seeing a man drive a wagon in new clothes. If he merely changed his worn clothes for other worn clothes it wouldn't make much difference.

But if he changed the wagon—maybe for a buggy—that would make a huge difference!

If anyone was trailing him, he'd ask about a man on a wagon. He might throw off a pursuer altogether by changing to a buggy.

Maybe he could get a buggy in the next town. He'd sell the wagon or abandon it. . . .

He reached the next settlement long after dark, when everything was closed up. It was a tiny place, half as large as the last. There was a general store, a blacksmith shop, and not much else. There was no telegraph and only a few other shacks, not even a saloon.

Cutler drove on through the burg and stopped in a grove of trees half a mile farther. He spent the night in the wagon again, and woke in the morning thinking he was getting too old for much more of this. His bones ached from the hard bed.

He picketed the horse in some grass and hiked back into the settlement. He bought food at the store and asked if anyone had a buggy for sale.

The store owner said, "Go ask Amos Timmins. Think he had a rig. . . . He's 'crost the road in that gray shack."

Cutler went across the road and rapped on the plank door of the shack. Amos Timmins, a man with a large belly and a straggly gray beard, said he had a buggy, and took Cutler around behind the shack to show him.

It was an ancient buggy, much of the leather scarred and

creased, but the wheels were in good shape and it was a one-horse vehicle. Timmins said he would grease the wheels and take twenty dollars for it.

Cutler offered fifteen, and they settled on eighteen.

Cutler explained that his horse was not far out of town, where he'd camped. Timmins then had a boy hook up the buggy; the lad drove Cutler back to his camp, and rode the horse back to the shack.

It took Cutler forever to get the heavy box into the back of the buggy. It was bulky, awkward, and obstinate. He moved the two vehicles as close together as he could get them and finally was able to shove, slide, and push the box from the wagon into the buggy, where it fitted tolerably well, sticking out only slightly. He roped it securely and covered it with the canvas, hoping no one would think it suspicious.

He might sell the wagon for a few dollars if he hung around the little burg long enough, but quickly decided against it; he would take the loss. He covered the wagon with brush and walked out to the road. It was invisible from there.

Satisfied, he drove on in the buggy.

Cutler had not shaved since the morning before he'd come into possession of the box. Now his beard was bristly, dark, and gray and felt a quarter of an inch long, and itchy. Scratching it, he smiled. It would help with his camouflage. If anyone was trailing him, and knew who they followed, they might not recognize him now. For years he had been clean-shaven in a land where most men wore facial hair. But it did itch abominably.

The road was winding down, toward the great valley; the mountains were spreading out, with gentler slopes. When he came to places where there were long vistas, he could see houses in the distance, with smoke rising. This was cattle and farming land.

In the middle of the day he came to a little town called Albers. A sign by the side of the road proclaimed that

117

Albers had a population of 978 and was horse country. Cutler wondered if they changed the figure every time a child was born.

The town was more like those he was used to. He left the buggy behind a saloon and went inside for a rest and a few beers. It was a dark, narrow room with a long bar and tables, nearly empty at this hour. The bartender and another man were playing checkers and paid him no mind.

Cutler took his beer to a side table and put his feet up. When he finished the beer he would ask the bartender how far it was to San Francisco. He must be well along by now. His sister would be astonished to see him. . . . They exchanged letters usually about once a year.

It was nice and warm in the saloon; the warmth and the beer made him a little sleepy—he hadn't had a decent night's rest since he got on the road. He pulled his shapeless hat down a little and dozed.

He didn't hear the two men come into the saloon, but in a few minutes he woke, hearing voices. He peered at them under the hat brim. Both were stocky men, dark and travel-stained. They glanced at him and perched on the rail, asking for whiskey. The barman put a bottle in front of them.

One asked, "You seen a man with a wagon come through here?"

The bartender shook his head. "Don't get out on the street much, gents, not durin' the day. You ought to ask at the stable, jus' down the street."

"We already done that." The two finished their drinks and went out.

Cutler chewed his lower lip. They were looking for him!

One of them looked like Jake Higgins, the saloon owner in Carson City. The other was probably the carpenter, Smitty. He had been in Jake's saloon a few times and had seen the man around town. How had they heard about him? It gave him a strange feeling to be the object of a search. Thank God they thought he still had the wagon.

And because of the beard they hadn't recognized him! Sitting there with his feet up, he probably looked like some saloon hanger-on.

He sat up and finished the beer, then stayed where he was for another hour, sopping up two more beers. Later he went out to the buggy and leaned on it, thinking. There was only one road through the town. Another road crossed it at right angles in the middle of the burg, but petered out quickly in both directions.

What should he do? With Jake and Smitty after him, he had best not go on. Were they capable of killing him for the box? No sense taking the chance of finding out.

He got in the rig, slapped the reins, and turned back the way he had come.

Who else was looking for him?

Smitty and Jake Higgins had picked a road over the mountains, and had thought they had the right one. A few people had told them a man on a wagon had come that way.

Of course the country was full of wagons. Every farmer had one or two, some householders had one, usually every storekeeper had one. . . .

But when they got as far as Albers, no one had seen a man on a wagon. Not a stranger, at any rate.

"We taken the wrong road," Smitty said. "He didn't come this way."

Jake had to agree. But he didn't want to go back. "Let's go on and cut across country when we get on the flats. Maybe we'll pick 'im up there."

Smitty nodded. To go back was to admit defeat. They might as well go home and forget it. "All right."

When Laredo and Pete Torres came to the fork in the road they halted and debated it. Should they continue on the main road to San Francisco, or take the smaller fork?

"What would you do if you were being followed?" Laredo looked at Pete.

119

"I might take the left fork."

"You *might*?"

"I think I would. I'd think I was throwing off a pursuer, if I were Cutler."

"You think Cutler knows he's being followed?"

"I think he'd have to assume it. He's not stupid."

Laredo nodded. "I think you're right. Let's take the left fork."

But they lost the quarry at Albers. No one they could find had seen a man on a wagon pass through town recently. Not a stranger. Had he holed up somewhere? There were plenty of places.

Laredo pointed out the dozen or more chairs scattered along the main street where men sat during the day, discussing everyone who came along.

Pete said, "Maybe he came through at night."

"How much night travel would he do—with a million dollars in the wagon bed?"

"Who would know that?"

"Well, he'd be nervous about it, wouldn't he? Let's backtrack and see if we've missed something."

Pete nodded. "And one other thing. He could have friends or kin around here, and he's visiting them."

Laredo smiled. "Would they ask him what he's got on the wagon?"

"Depends on what kind of friends, I suppose."

They went back to a tiny little place with no name. It had only a general store and a blacksmith shop. They asked the store owner about a man on a wagon. The owner said he hadn't seen such a man. Neither had the blacksmith.

"He still could have come through at night," Pete insisted. "No one would have seen him."

"Let's go back to the next town."

They returned to the tiny settlement just past the fork in the road. The livery stable owner had seen such a man, yes. He slept in his wagon behind the store. Given him two bits for oats.

"Where did he go?"

The man pointed down the road. "Toward Albers."

"Thanks." They went into the restaurant and ordered food. Laredo said, "We lost him between here and Albers. Did he turn off?"

"I don't remember seeing a road between here and the little burg."

"Let's make sure this time."

There was no road, not even a trail they could find until they got to the general store again. The owner repeated what he'd said before. He had not seen a man on a wagon.

The blacksmith suggested they talk to his brother-in-law, Amos. "Maybe he saw 'im." He pointed. "He lives in 'at there gray shack."

Amos nodded to them. Yes, he had seen a man. Not on a wagon, but he had sold a pilgrim a buggy.

"A buggy!" Laredo said with a laugh. "Of course! No wonder nobody has seen a man on a wagon—he's got a buggy!"

Amos said, "Told me he was camped outside of town. I dunno if he had a wagon or not. He said he had a horse."

"Did he ride the horse into town?"

"No. He was hikin'."

Pete asked, "How did he get the buggy to where the horse was?"

Amos grinned. "I sent m'boy along and he brought back my horse."

"Can we talk to the boy?"

"Sure." Amos went into the shack and came back with the lad. Yes, the stranger had had a horse all right. And a wagon too.

Laredo asked, "Did he have anything on the wagon?"

"Something. But there was a old canvas over it."

They thanked the boy and Amos and rode out of town, looking for the spot Cutler had camped. They found the wagon quickly, covered with brush.

Pete said, "He only had one horse so he left this here. Buying the buggy proves he knows he was followed."

121

"That's right. So did he go on past Albers in the buggy, or did he turn back?"

"Why would he turn back?"

"To get on the main road to San Francisco."

"But if he turned back he might meet whoever's following him."

Laredo nodded. "Unless he changed his appearance so they wouldn't recognize him."

Pete smiled. "It makes sense. But what did he do? I think we'll have to go back to Albers and ask questions."

"I'm afraid so."

Frank Slater left Dallas and headed north instead of south. He had talked about getting a job for a year, but the million dollars was too much of a magnet. He could not stay away.

He turned the horse's head toward Carson City and arrived there, by good planning, long after dark. He went directly to his shack on Cutler's land.

Striking a match, he was immediately in a rage that someone had wrecked the inside of the house. It had been somewhat cleaned up—he found a lantern in working order and lit it—but the bed ropes were still cut and the shelves knocked down.

He brought in his blanket roll and spent the night sleeping on the hard floor, cursing whoever had cut the bed ropes.

But in the morning light he had a shock. The woodpile had been entirely removed! Every stick of it was gone—and so was the metal box.

It had been discovered! He had lost a million dollars! Slater sat down on the ground and cried.

But as he stared at the spot where the woodpile had been, thought stirred within him. The wood belonged to Cutler. As a matter of fact, he, Slater, had cut the wood for Cutler's fireplace. So Cutler had come for it . . . and found the box. It was the obvious solution. Cutler had it!

He saddled his horse and rode into town at once, and

found Cutler's dry goods store closed up. He asked neighboring store owners. No one knew where Cutler had gone; they were all as surprised as he. One morning the store had been found locked and Cutler was not in his home.

Slater knew why. He had the damned shipment box!

But where had he gone?

He quickly learned that Cutler had a wagon he used in his business. So Cutler had loaded the box on the wagon and skipped out. He had hit the road, but which one?

To Slater there was only one place Cutler would go. San Francisco. Of course there were many roads, but if Slater went to Frisco, he might stumble on the man. He knew Cutler by sight.

It was his best bet. He headed south at once.

But before he had gone five miles he met Turk Jessop, who just returned from Reno.

On recognizing Slater, Jessop pulled a pistol and fired.

Chapter Fourteen

Turk Jessop's third shot creased the rump of Slater's horse, and the animal reared suddenly. Slater was tossed off like a rag doll. He rolled into the weeds, tugging out his pistol. On his belly, he fired two shots at the advancing horseman—before Jessop's fifth shot slammed into his chest. He jerked and dropped the revolver, doubling up slowly.

Jessop rode up close and got down to pull the other's head around. Slater's eyes were glazing over.

Jessop snapped, "Where's the box?"

Slater opened his eyes to slits; Turk was only a misty blur.

Jessop growled. "Dammit, where's the goddam box?" He shook Slater. "Come on. . . ."

He was annoyed with himself. He shouldn't have let his anger get the best of him. He should have gotten the drop and forced the information out of him.

Damn, now Slater was dying. . . .

He said again more urgently, "Frank—where's the box?"

Was there a smile on Slater's pale face? Maybe a ghost of a smile. He whispered, ". . . in the . . . woodpile . . ."

Then he was gone.

Jessop shook him again, watching the man's eyes widen. Shit! Slater was finished. Jessop stood, swearing great oaths. What the hell did that mean, "In the woodpile"?

He sighed, staring down at the man he'd killed. Dammit! He'd let his anger get the better of him again, and now a million dollars had flown away.

He bent down and searched the body. Maybe Slater had something written down. But there was nothing. Very little money and no papers. Slater had been a pauper. Probably his horse and gun were all he owned.

Jessop took a few steps. He had outfoxed himself. In the woodpile? What woodpile? Had Slater hidden the box in a woodpile somewhere? There must be thousands of woodpiles in the country. Every house had one. Jessop shook his head in defeat. He had been too quick to shoot.

Reloading the pistol, he glanced around. He was miles from town and it was a sure bet no one had seen or heard the shooting. No one appeared at any rate. What should he do with the body and the horse? He holstered the pistol and got out the makin's to roll a cigarette. An hour ago he had had none of these problems. Well, if he had a rope he could tie the body on the horse and send it along toward town for someone to find. But he had no rope, and neither did Slater.

The next best thing was to drag the body into the brush and lead the horse away. Sooner or later both would be found, but he would be far away by then. He gave another look around, puffed on the cigarette, and dropped it, to grind it into the dirt with his boot heel. Then he dragged the body off the trail and gathered up the reins of the horse.

What the hell did "in the woodpile" mean? And why would Slater hide the box in one? Had Slater been lying to him as he died? Maybe he hadn't realized he was near death. That was very possible.

He mounted his own gelding and turned south on the road, leading Slater's animal. Was the box gone forever? What had happened to Shorty? Had Slater been on his way to meet him—or had Shorty grabbed the box in a double cross, leaving Slater to hold the bag?

If those two had stolen the box from him, Jessop, why would not one of them steal it from the other?

Now all he had to do was find Shorty.

The one thing he was sure of, Shorty had not gone to Reno. He, Jessop, had just come from there and he hadn't passed anyone he knew on the road. Maybe Shorty had taken the box to San Francisco to get it open.

He turned Slater's horse loose in a grassy little valley and never looked back.

A half-dozen people in Albers had seen a man with a buggy. When Laredo questioned them closely, one man was positive the stranger had gone east from Albers, back the way he had come. The others weren't sure.

Pete asked the man, "Why are you so sure?"

"Because I was sitting there on that bench, waiting for my old man to come out of the leather shop." The man pointed to a bench. "I saw this gent come into town with 'is buggy and later I seen him go out."

"The same man?"

"Yes, the same man. And the same buggy. He had a piece of canvas over something that stuck out in the back of the buggy, like a trunk."

Laredo looked at Pete. "I think that's the buggy."

They thanked the man, got on the horses, and rode east toward the fork.

Cutler was not at all sure he had thrown his pursuers off the track. He kept looking over his shoulder—to see no one there. There was so much at stake. He was well aware that his life would be worth little more than an old peach seed if someone wanted to take the box away from him. He was not a gunman—he was not even armed. The someone would shoot him down and that would be that.

But of course a million dollars was worth the risk.

Only, could he stay ahead of them? Horsemen could easily overtake a man in a buggy. Could he get to San Francisco before they overtook him?

Probably not. At least he would be smart to figure it that way. *If* someone was behind him, they were sure to catch up. He ought to get off the main road again, maybe wait it all out. Had he gone off half-cocked in the first place? Without thinking it through? Probably. The riches in the steel box had blinded him. He should have made better plans.

But now that he was out on the road and committed—what should he do? There was no possibility of turning back—he'd only run into them.

So he had better turn off again. But where? He would have to go to a settled community. He was no hand at camping out, or surviving in the wild; not for any length of time, say a week.

But if he suddenly appeared in a settled town, everyone within miles would learn about him in a matter of days. Gossip would spread word about the stranger, and if there was a newspaper, it would print the item as well.

It wouldn't be that way if he were some young drifter, looking for odd jobs. He was middle-aged, after all, and had a certain dignity. They were more likely to imagine he had murdered his wife or partner and was running from the law.

Cutler shook his head to clear it. He was putting the worst possible face on it, wasn't he?

There was a large dust cloud ahead. He peered at it, wondering if it meant danger. And then, as he approached, he saw it was a small herd of horses, being driven by several young boys. They were coming along the road toward him, but suddenly turned off toward the east.

As Cutler reached the spot, where three pines stood in a friendly clump, he saw it was a road of sorts. It curled away from the main road, toward the distant hills.

Almost without thinking, he pulled on the reins and turned to follow the herd.

He had to slow to a walk. The horse herd was in no hurry. Stretching away on either side were weedy fields with clumps of trees here and there, with no fences anywhere. Possibly land that no one owned. It did not look as if it had ever been plowed.

Seeing the horses reminded him of Jack Brodie. Brodie had been a horse nut, always talking, when they'd been partners, about owning a horse ranch one day. He and Brodie had started a business together, but could seldom agree on anything.

Brodie had been much too willing, Cutler thought, to take the shady road when it was available. He was not really crooked, but he bent a bit too much.

That was a laugh. What would Brodie think of him now, with a million dollars of Uncle Sam's money in the back of the buggy? Well, of course Brodie would be for it. Would want to cut himself in.

They had stumbled along in the business for a year or more, quarreling and grumbling, and had finally called it quits. But he had missed Brodie after they parted. He had been a jovial sort, slow to anger, but willing to argue. . . .

Then Brodie had come into a little money. An uncle had died and Jack was the only kin. He had withdrawn from the partnership and had bought a horse ranch near the town of Hammet.

Hammet.

It couldn't be too far from where he was now. He had never been there but he recalled Jack talking about it. Would Jack put him up for a time? Of course he would, for old time's sake if nothing else.

What excuse would he use? That he was out looking for a piece of property to buy. He'd sold the store and wanted to settle down—he was getting on. Brodie would believe that.

And it would solve his problem. He would lose his pursuers for good and all.

He came to a little town called Manley and got directions from a young man digging a ditch. Hammet was about sixty miles farther on, south and east, in the foothills.

It took three days to get there, because he got lost for nearly a day and had to backtrack. Jack Brodie's ranch was west of the town, so he did not enter it. Brodie's mailbox was on the rutted cart track that passed as a road. It read J. BRODIE.

A trail led into the hills, and in half an hour Cutler could see smoke rising from a house. Was Jack married?

He was not. And he was astonished to see Cutler.

"For God's sake! Where did you drop from?" Brodie was a thickset man, as old as Cutler but deeply tanned, with a black mustache and heavy brows.

"I came to visit an old friend."

"Well, Jesus Christ! I don't believe it." He gave Cutler a hand down from the buggy. "You came all the way from Carson City just to visit me? How the hell did you find me?"

"You wrote me where you were—you forget?"

"Yeh, I guess I did. Well, come on in. I got some coffee boiling."

The house was more than a shack; it was solidly built, with a fireplace and a fieldstone chimney. The furniture was old and heavy, however, and Brodie wasn't much of a housekeeper.

Brodie set out two cups and poured into them from the metal coffeepot. "Who's keeping the store f'you?"

"I sold out. The whole shebang. I'm gettin' too old to argue with folks any longer. I just want to settle down like you did."

Brodie laughed. "It ain't all that easy. I'm gettin' by, but there's a lot of work. . . . You're lookin' good, Pete."

"I feel fine." He drank the coffee. "Guess I better unhook the buggy. You going to ask me t'stay the night?"

"Of course you'll stay the night. All week if you want. I ain't had a soul t'talk to since last time I was in town."

Cutler got up and went out to the buggy. He unhitched the horse as Brodie opened the corral gate. They put the horse inside. Brodie forked some hay into a trough.

"You got a valise in the buggy?"

Cutler shook his head. "I didn't bring anything with me. Travelin' light." It sounded a little lame to him—nobody went on a long trip without a suitcase of some kind. It was something he hadn't thought of. He hoped Brodie wouldn't notice. He saw the other looking at the bulge the steel box made, but Brodie said nothing. They left the buggy sitting in the yard in front of the house and went back inside.

At the door Cutler paused and looked back at the buggy. It would be safe enough there. Brodie never had visitors, apparently. He'd said he hadn't talked to anyone since he last went to town.

Brodie noticed the look. If Pete had sold the store, and everything he owned, he probably had the cash with him. Maybe in that bulge in the buggy. . . .

Chapter Fifteen

THEY were a long way behind Cutler. Maybe as much as a week because of all the backtracking and making sure. Now they were reasonably certain Cutler had taken this particular road toward San Francisco and was driving a buggy. They passed several men driving wagons, and one said yes, he'd passed a man in a black buggy a day or two ago.

Laredo asked, "The man was alone?"

"Yep. Nobody with 'im."

However, when they reached the town of Bloomfield, no one had seen a stranger in a buggy. They spent several hours asking questions and at the end of it were fairly certain Cutler had not been in the town.

"He turned off again," Pete said, disgusted. "He is sure making work for us."

"He's worried," Laredo replied. "That box is wearing him down. We've got to go back."

They followed a trail that led off to the west and it ended up at an abandoned mine.

A dozen miles farther on, a road branched off toward

the west and they turned into it, heading toward distant foothills.

When they came to the town of Manley, three people had seen a stranger in a buggy. One of them was able to describe Cutler, and two said that something had bulged out the back of the buggy.

It was Cutler, all right.

That evening they discussed land. Cutler said he was looking to buy a piece of property with a house on it. He wanted something with fruit trees and good ground for a garden, and enough land for some cattle.

"There's lots of land," Brodie said. "There's a widow woman lives over east, ten miles or so, got a nice small ranch. Don't know what she'd take for it, but you could ask. The talk is, she wants to go into town to live since her husband died."

"Might be what I'm looking for."

They had another cup of coffee then Cutler wanted to turn in. He was tired from the long trip.

Brodie had a small spare bedroom at the back of the house. It had a brass bed, a chest of drawers, and a chair. The privy was out behind the house. He lit a lantern and showed Cutler in.

"There's a spare blanket if you need it. . . ."

Brodie sat in the parlor while Cutler came in from the privy and got into bed. In an hour he stood at the door and listened to his guest's regular breathing. Cutler was fast asleep.

Then Brodie took a lantern and went outside to look in the buggy.

He lifted the canvas and stared at the metal box. Cutler had a goddam safe! It had a strange-looking lock, deeply recessed and probably strong. Doubtless all Cutler's cash was in it, and that might be a goodly amount. The safe was heavy as hell.

He searched the buggy, looking for the key, and found nothing. Cutler hadn't hidden it there. He went back in the house and listened to Cutler's breathing, then searched his clothes. No key. Not even in his boots.

Where the hell was it?

Cutler must have it in a very clever place. Maybe it was somewhere in this room . . . but a cursory search did not turn it up. He went back through the house and looked everywhere Cutler had been. He even went out to the privy and searched it.

Frustration.

It was very late, so he went to bed. But he could not sleep. Where the hell was Cutler's key? He would have to go over the buggy again in daylight—when Cutler was not around. Maybe he could arrange that.

Did Cutler have any kin? He dimly remembered him saying something about a sister . . . but could not recall if she was alive or not. His wife was dead. No, Cutler was probably alone in the world. Who would miss him? He had gotten the impression that no one knew where Cutler had gone.

If no one knew where Cutler was, and he had no kin to ask questions, maybe he, Brodie, might come into a lot of money all of a sudden.

Did he have the nerve to do it?

He drifted off to sleep thinking about money, a pile of money, the kind of money he'd never had.

In the morning after an early breakfast, he had his chores. And as he went about the rounds, he thought about Cutler—about all the times they'd argued and fought, about all the things that annoyed him about the man.

By noontime he was growly and gruff when he came back to the house. Cutler asked him, "What the matter? You feel all right?"

"Yeh . . ." Brodie realized his feelings were showing too much. He'd have to conceal them or Cutler would get defensive, and might even pack up and go. He made some excuse and managed a smile.

After lunch he asked Cutler if he'd like to see the ranch. Cutler agreed and Brodie saddled another horse in the barn.

133

Then he strapped on a revolver, and as he slid a rifle into the saddle boot Cutler asked him, "Why the guns?"

"In case we see a wolf. They pull down the young foals if they get a chance. You got a gun?"

"No."

"Well, you won't need one. We may not see any." Brodie looked at the sky. "There's coyotes too, but they don't bother the horses." He mounted. "They talkin' in town about putting a bounty on the wolves. . . . Hope they do."

The house and barn were surrounded by barbed wire, to keep the stock from trampling his garden, Brodie said. He got down and opened the gate, then put it up again when they went through. He had a small reservoir, fed by a spring; it was several hundred yards from the barn. Beyond it was a small forest. The trees marched down from the hills, not far away, providing, Brodie said, a source of firewood.

"I jus' snake a wagon in there and cut out the fallen stuff, nice'n dry. Do that about every couple of months and I got plenty of wood for the stove."

Cutler said, "You don't have to go to town for much."

"Well, for staples, flour, sugar, coffee . . . and t'see a newspaper now'n then . . . maybe talk to a few folks. Neighbors don't come by very often. Ever'body busy working."

"I guess so." Cutler nodded.

Brodie pointed out his horse herd, a hundred or so animals cropping grass in a green meadow. They rode around the herd, into the shelter of the pines. It was hilly there and Brodie explained that he had half a dozen cows and sometimes they wandered into the hills and he had to go chouse them out.

"Don't see any today. . . . Keep your eye peeled. I d'want 'em in here. One of 'em could break a leg. . . ."

"You ought t'put bells on them."

"That's a good idea. Guess I should." Brodie halted. He motioned to Cutler. In a whisper he said, "Thought I saw something slinking in that brush." He pointed.

134

Cutler stood in the stirrups, peering at the spot. "Don't see anything. . . ."

Brodie swung down and pulled the rifle from the boot. He motioned again. "Ride up there slow. I'll go around thisaway." He levered a shell into the chamber.

Cutler nudged the horse as Brodie hurried off to the right on foot. In a few moments Cutler was in shoulder-high brush, pushing through, trying not to cough. Then the brush thinned out and he was through it, glancing around to see a wolf—

Brodie was behind him, to Cutler's right. He fired and the shot hit Cutler just behind the ear. He fell like a heavy sack of meal and the horse skittered.

Gritting his teeth, Brodie levered another shell into the Winchester and ran to the body, ready to fire again. But it wasn't necessary. Cutler had no pulse at all. The lead had smashed the skull.

Brodie went back for his horse and tied the two animals to a branch. Then he sat down, facing away from the body, and rolled a cigarette with shaking fingers.

He had done it.

He finished the cigarette, then got up and made himself search the body for the key. He took off Cutler's boots and felt through them, he examined every stitch of clothing, even tore the shapeless hat apart. Nothing.

Where the hell was the key? What would Cutler be packing a steel box around for, if he didn't have the key?

Well then, it had to be hidden in the buggy.

He swung up on the horse and rode back to the house. He pulled the buggy around the house and into the barn, just in case someone happened by. Then he found an old blanket, took a shovel, and rode back out to the spot. There he dug a deep hole beside the body.

He rolled Cutler's remains in the blanket and pulled the bundle into the hole. He never in his life had figured he'd be doing this. He filled in the dirt and tamped it down, scattering the rest of it around so there'd be no mound. He kicked leaves and twigs over the spot till it looked undisturbed. No one would ever find Cutler now.

Riding back to the barn, he searched the buggy again. He could find no key. How clever could Cutler be?

He had to get rid of the buggy of course. He couldn't sell it so he had to smash it up somehow. Why not take it apart and bury the pieces? He would give it a very good search as he took it apart piece by piece.

The ground was fairly soft beside the barn so he took two hours digging a big square hole, five or six feet deep. Then, examining each inch, he took the buggy apart, beginning with the varnished cloth top. He hacksawed it up and tossed the pieces in the hole.

It took three days to take it all apart. He had to smash the wheels with a heavy mallet, taking out each spoke . . . but there was no key. He ripped the seat to shreds, sifting through every tuft of horsehair. No key.

When every bit of cloth and metal was in the hole, he still had not found the key. He *knew* the key had not been hidden in the buggy. He filled in the hole and piled some old corn cribs on the spot.

He sat on a box and stared at the steel safe with its smeary brown paint. Now what would he do?

There was only one thing. He had to take it somewhere, to someone who could open it. He had a feeling an ordinary locksmith would not be the man.

Was it possible that Cutler had not had a key?

He went in the house and examined again the bedroom Cutler had slept in. He took the room apart, but found nothing.

Why in hell would Cutler be packing around a steel box he couldn't open? Cutler had said he had sold his land and the store and was looking for something to buy. But there was no money on him. It *had* to be in the goddam box!

It was the most baffling thing Brodie had ever encountered.

136

It was totally frustrating. He wished he could bring Cutler back to life to answer *one* question.

The town of Hammet was three times as large as Manley and some sixty miles farther on, Laredo learned. He and Pete had a beer and some lunch and rode on. Cutler had come through Manley, that was sure.

But he had not arrived in Hammet.

Or if he had, he was invisible. None of the porch sitters had seen him. There had been men with wagons and others in buggies, but no stranger in a black buggy. He had not stopped in any of the stores or in the two hotels. No one had seen a stranger with a cart or any contraption that was capable of hauling a box.

"Unless he got it open," Pete said.

"Between here and Manley?"

"Yeah, not likely. That means he stopped off somewhere between here and Manley. He had to."

Laredo inquired about roads that turned off the main one to Manley, and was told there were two. One went to a small lake where there was a tiny settlement, the other petered out after a few miles.

They investigated both. There was a small general store at the lake and nothing else except a dozen houses and shacks. The storekeeper was an old man, hard of hearing, but his eyesight was excellent. He was absolutely positive that he'd seen no stranger in a buggy.

The other road served a rancher and went only a few hundred yards past his house. The rancher's wife had seen no one at all for weeks.

There was nothing to do but go back to the town. They sat in a saloon over beers. "He's staying with somebody," Pete said. "Where else would he go?"

"Up in the hills, camping out?"

Pete shrugged. "Maybe, but I doubt it. He's probably got a relative living around here somewhere."

"And there's one other thing. . . ."

"What?"

"No matter where he goes, people are going to wonder about the steel box. Can he conceal it in the buggy?"

Pete nodded, sipping the beer. "Maybe . . ."

"But speaking of relatives, I wonder who he might know. Why don't we wire Reinhardt to find out more about Mr. Cutler for us?"

"Good idea."

They borrowed some paper from the bartender and composed a wire, then walked to the telegraph office with it.

A reply from Reinhardt came in about five hours. As far as he could discover, Cutler had no kin except a sister living in San Francisco. He could not find out her name or if she was married. Cutler had owned the dry goods store alone but he had once been in business with a man named Jack Brodie. Reinhardt could not find out what had happened to Brodie.

"That's interesting," Laredo said, "a partner, huh?"

"We can ask the postmaster if there's a Brodie in this neck of the woods."

"Let's go."

The postmaster owned a photographer's shop and used part of his office for the mail. He smiled when they asked him about Brodie.

"Sure, I know Jack. He lives out of town—got a horse ranch. You friends of his?"

"In a way," Laredo said. "Which road?"

"Go west, past the holding corrals, and stay on the road. His name is on the postbox."

When they were outside, Laredo said, "Eureka!"

Chapter Sixteen

THEY rode past the corrals as the postmaster had directed, and an hour later came to the postbox with the name J. Brodie. The track to the house curved away to the right. They could not see the house.

Laredo said, "Let's slip up on it. If Cutler's there maybe we'll see the buggy."

They made a wide circle, and when the roofline of a building came into sight, got down and slipped closer like Apaches, till they had a good view of the ranch house and a row of stables.

"Nobody around," Pete said. "Don't see any chimney smoke."

"And no buggy."

"It could be in a stable."

"Could be."

Pete said, "Let's ride in like pilgrims. Brodie may be asleep or drunk."

But he was neither. No one was in the house or in any of the stables. There was no buggy anywhere. The house was unlocked and there was evidence that someone had searched the house—drawers left open and things on shelves tumbled about.

"Something's happened here," Laredo said. "But how long ago?"

Pete examined the kitchen. "Somebody went through the cans and bottles. . . . Maybe Cutler and Brodie went off together."

"In the buggy?"

"Well, it's not here."

Laredo scratched his chin. "From the descriptions of it, would Cutler's buggy carry two men, the steel box, and whatever they took from the house?"

Pete made a face. "Sounds like a full load."

"There's no wagon anywhere around. Did you ever see a ranch without a wagon?"

"No. Never did. And plenty of wheel marks around the stables."

"Maybe Cutler was here and left."

Pete rolled a cigarette. "And Brodie left too? Did he take the wagon? If they left together, would they take both?"

"A lot of questions, *amigo*."

They rode back into town, to the telegraph office, and wired Reinhardt, telling him what they'd found and that they suspected Cutler and Brodie had left together. Lawmen should be notified, with a description of both, that they were wanted for questioning.

There were half a dozen roads and trails out of Hammet, a bartender told them, most good enough for a buggy or wagon. But Brodie had not been seen in the town—so said those questioned.

Maybe he had gone back toward San Francisco.

As for Cutler, he had simply disappeared. Pete suggested Brodie was not the only person Cutler knew. Maybe he was in hiding with someone else.

"Is that likely?"

Pete shrugged. "What's your idea?"

"Well, he was in possession of more than a million dollars. What if Brodie found out about it?"

"Would Cutler tell him?"

"Just having the steel box would be suspicious...."

"Ummm."

"How do we know what their relationship was?"

Pete thought about it. "Cutler's trail ends after Manley —he never got as far as Hammet, according to all the people we've talked to." He looked meaningfully at Laredo. "If he went to Brodie's ranch...maybe he's still there."

"Six feet underground?"

"Maybe."

Laredo smiled grimly. "Plenty of folks would do murder for that kind of money."

Pete nodded, and a faraway look came into his dark eyes. "If Brodie did kill him for the box, he's due for a surprise."

"That's right. He can't open it."

They wired Reinhardt again, telling him of their suspicions, then rode back to Brodie's ranch. It was an extensive spread, only part of it fenced. Part was thick pine woods that had probably never been thinned. They rode over the ranch, hoping to find evidences of a fresh grave, but did not. Of course, as Pete said, it would not be too difficult to conceal it. And it was impossible for only two of them to search the woods inside of a month.

They found no grave...and no buggy.

At the town of Demster, as they rode back toward Carson City, they wired Reinhardt again for news. The Treasury agent's return wire was quick. The steel box had been located! And Jack Brodie with it!

Brodie had been stopped in the town of Loganville by a deputy who thought he resembled the description: a man on a wagon, with a steel box in the wagon bed. He had found the box when he pulled off the canvas that covered it.

141

Also, he had found a letter addressed to J. Brodie in the man's coat.

"Careless," Pete said.

Brodie was now in the Loganville jail.

Reinhardt's wire seemed to express his elation. He asked them to go to Loganville, to bring Brodie and the shipment box back to Carson City.

The map showed Loganville to be about forty miles to the south. It took them almost two days over terrible roads to reach it. The town was small but sprawling. It spread itself over the slope of a gentle hill. The jail was built of fieldstones and cement, with a log roof. They tied the horses at the hitchrack and went inside.

The deputy, the only law in town, was Will Tretta, a slim young man with a cherubic face. He read their credentials and nodded, apparently impressed.

Laredo asked, "Has Brodie said anything to you?"

"Yep. Said he hasn't done anything."

Pete asked, "Where's the steel box?"

Tretta pointed. "Under my desk." He kicked it. "What's in it anyways?"

"Securities. Let's talk to Brodie."

"Sure." The deputy indicated the jail door. "Right through there."

The jail had only two cells, each with two bunks. Brodie was the only prisoner. He sat on one of the lower bunk beds and stared at them as they entered. He was unshaven and looked very seedy.

Laredo leaned against the bars. "Hullo, Brodie."

"Who're you?"

"My name's Laredo and this is Pete Torres. We're going to take you back to Carson City to stand trial. . . ."

"Stand trial for what?"

"Robbery—and maybe murder."

Brodie jumped up. "I never murdered nobody!"

"But you admit you stole the box?"

"I don't admit nothing!"

Pete said, "You were in possession of the box."

142

"I don't even know what's in it!"

Laredo asked, "Where did you get it?"

Brodie shook his head.

"You don't know?"

Brodie shook his head again.

Pete said, "It just jumped up on his wagon and covered itself with some canvas. Very cooperative box."

Brodie glared at him.

Laredo asked, "Where were you going?"

Brodie stared and said nothing. He turned his face away.

The deputy was in the doorway. "He don't talk much."

"All right," Laredo said. "Open the cell. We'll be on our way."

"You want me to cuff him?" The deputy grinned. "I got some leg irons."

"No, don't bother."

"He'll try to get away. . . ." Tretta selected a key from a large ring and slid it into the lock.

"He can try," Laredo said. "No one said whether they wanted him dead or alive, so he's got a choice." To Brodie he said, "Get your coat."

Brodie's wagon was in the stable behind the jail. They carried the heavy box out and dropped it into the wagon bed and pulled the canvas over it. Pete motioned Brodie onto the seat. "You'll drive the nag."

They left Loganville behind and headed north.

Deputy Tretta mentioned, over coffee with Dan Winegar, who owned and ran *The Loganville Ledger*, that he had apprehended a criminal named Jack Brodie who was suspected of robbery and murder. Loganville hadn't had a murder in two years and very little robbery. Brodie was news.

But there was more. Two important government agents had come for Brodie, so he was doubtless a big-time criminal, though the agents had said very little. The steel box that Brodie had when he was arrested was probably filled with important government documents.

Winegar agreed, and did an article about it for the paper.

The fact that government agents were interested in the event caused the item to be picked up by other newspapers.

Fritz Benner noticed the story as he scanned the half-dozen newspapers he looked at each day. The box had come to light!

He yelled for Abner Parker.

Within the hour, Abner was on his horse hurrying toward Loganville.

Chapter Seventeen

JACK Brodie had ideas of escape. Carson City was a long
way off, and he had no intention of going there. He could
probably not get away with the box, but he could make off
with his life. They might find Cutler's body, after all. Such
things were possible.

They were two to his one, but they seemed very casual.
They talked and joked between themselves and paid almost
no attention to him. Sometimes they rode ahead of him and
sometimes behind. Brodie was stoic. He said nothing to
them unless it was absolutely necessary, attending only to
his reins. Maybe they would think he had decided his cause
was hopeless.

The first night they made camp by a small stream, in the
middle of nowhere. They had not seen a habitation all that
day and had passed no one on the road.

Laredo, he thought, was the leader of the two, and
talked pleasantly with him, though Brodie answered with
grunts most times. Pete was very reserved, looking at him
from under heavy black brows.

They both made supper over a small bed of coals, mostly broiling meat on sharp sticks.

When they rolled in their blankets for the night, Brodie lay perfectly still, wide-awake. This was a good place from which to quietly slip away. There were hundreds of good hiding places. He would hole up somewhere till they got tired of looking for him.

Several hours passed and the only sounds were the occasional crackle of the dying fire and the far-off hoots of owls.

Brodie sat up slowly and reached for his boots.

Then he froze. Loud and sharply clear came the unmistakable click-clack of a revolver hammer being drawn back. No word was spoken.

Brodie lay down again, his heart pounding.

Jesus! Maybe they did know what they were doing!

In the morning nothing at all was said about the incident. They made breakfast and rode on, paying him no more attention than they had the day before.

Brodie began to feel that the game was up. They would pin the robbery of the box on him—unless he could think of a very good story. Could he say he'd found it? That sounded awkward. But if he once admitted he'd gotten it from Cutler they would never let him rest till he'd told them all of it. Could he say that Cutler had left it with him? Would that sound plausible? No, why would Cutler leave his life savings with someone else? And the next question they would ask was—where did Cutler go? They would never believe him if he said he didn't know.

Maybe it would be best never to admit he'd seen Cutler. But then, how had he come into possession of the box?

The box was the damning thing! It connected him to Cutler. He should have buried it with Cutler and dug it up in a year or two. He should have.

What was in the box, anyway? And why should two government agents be interested in it? When he asked them, they shook their heads. Was it possible it didn't contain Cutler's money—but maybe government money? That was a new idea to him. It explained a lot. . . .

And it worried him too. The government could bring the weight of the law down on him and crush him. . . . But they couldn't make him talk if he refused. Torture was out!

But he'd have to be on his guard that they didn't trick him into saying something about Cutler that he shouldn't.

He should have buried that goddam box with Cutler.

When they stopped for the night, Brodie felt terrible. He still hadn't figured out his defense. How could he get around having the damned box?

If he said nothing at all, refused to open his mouth, could they still convict him? Maybe, but the more he thought about it, that seemed his best idea, say nothing. If they were going to prove him guilty, let them damned well prove it.

Laredo felt sure they had Cutler's murderer. But they had no body. "Will a court convict him without a corpse?"

Pete shrugged. "I guess it depends on the court. But he's got a good chance of sliding out of it. . . ."

"The body's buried somewhere on that ranch. It's got to be."

"I think so too."

"That damned box has caused a lot of deaths."

Pete nodded, watching Brodie rub down the horse; the man was good with animals. Laredo was right. They might not be able to hang him without a body. A good defense lawyer would say, "If he's guilty, show us a body."

In the middle of the afternoon they came to the little town of Gering. There was plenty of sun left, but Laredo said, "Why not get us a bath while we've got the chance?"

Pete agreed, and they dismounted in front of Gering House, a hotel that boasted seven rooms. A sign read: BATH AND SHAVE 35¢.

They flipped a coin and Pete won the first bath. Laredo and Brodie sat in the tiny room in front of the desk. Brodie stared out of the dusty window at the street, while Laredo read a newspaper that was only a week old. They got copies every Thursday, the clerk said. "They bring 'em over from the county seat."

Pete had to cut wood for the fire, then pour hot water into a big galvanized iron tub that had a wooden bottom and back. The soap was yellow and hard as a rock and made no suds. But he scrubbed himself and got out, dumped the water out, and rinsed the tub for the next occupant.

He put the same clothes back on and went out to the front. Laredo got up with a yawn and put the paper aside. A big man was just stepping down from his horse outside.

At that moment, when he thought Laredo's attention had strayed, Brodie jumped for the door. He rushed through it and ran full tilt into the big man—who grabbed him and held on as Brodie yelped.

Pete quickly disentangled Brodie from the other's grasp. "Thanks, friend."

The big man nodded. "What's goin' on?"

Laredo showed him a badge. "Just taking this man in."

"Oh, I see. That your wagon out there?"

Laredo nodded, thinking it an odd question. The big man smiled and signed the register and clumped upstairs. When he had gone, Laredo looked at the ledger. The man had signed as Abner Parker. It meant nothing to him.

He took Pete aside. Pete had noticed the man's question.

"He's no friend of Brodie's. Is he interested in the wagon?"

"Seems to be."

"I think he made a mistake saying so."

"Yes, maybe he was surprised to see it." Laredo scratched his chin. "I'll take the bath quick as I can, then we ought to hightail it out of town. What you figure?"

Pete nodded, rolling a cigarette.

Brodie sat by the window glumly, frowning at Pete, who lolled in a chair, apparently paying him no attention.

The big man, Parker, came downstairs, nodded to Pete, and went out as Brodie glared at him. Parker mounted and rode slowly north as Pete watched from the doorway.

When Laredo returned from the bathhouse, they told the clerk they would be moving on and went out to the horses.

The sun was going down as they left the town behind; the land was rolling, with clumps of trees here and there, and as the sun disappeared they pulled off the road and stopped in a small wood, out of sight of the road.

They made a cold camp, ignoring Brodie's grumbling, and sometime during the night Laredo heard a horseman go by on the road. Was it Parker? Was the big man after the steel box? But how did he know about the box?

When he woke Pete for his watch, Pete said, "Somebody told him."

"Who?"

"Maybe Slater or Shorty. What happened to them?"

Laredo grunted. "Wish we knew."

The country was relatively flat and uninhabited as they rode on the next morning. They saw nothing at all of the big man, Parker. The wagon rumbled on, with a morose Brodie slumping on the seat. He seemed deep in his own thoughts.

Laredo scouted ahead for several hours, wondering about Parker. Was the man planning to ambush them to obtain the box?

At midday they came to a jumble of low hills and halted. This might be an ideal ambush spot. Pete pulled his rifle from the boot and levered a shell into the chamber.

"I'll take a look around. . . ."

He moved off to the right, skirting the hills, then disappeared behind a row of bushy trees.

Brodie spoke for the first time that day. He looked at Laredo. "You got the box. Let me go."

"Can't do that."

"Why not. Who's going to know?"

"We've already reported that you're in custody."

"Tell them you got the wrong man."

Laredo laughed. "We don't think so. What did you do with Cutler's body?"

"I didn't do anything to him."

"Then how did you come into possession of the box?"

Brodie stared at him.

"Well?"

"I got nothing to say t'you." Brodie lapsed into silence.

Pete appeared after an hour, half a mile away on a ridge. He waved, then disappeared again. Laredo said, "Let's go."

The rutted road wound into the hills. Laredo rode ahead of the wagon, the Winchester across his thighs. The hills were brown with grass, providing no cover. A few arroyos with crumbling edges flowed down into the road, but nothing moved except several hawks, high in the sky, circling, circling. . . .

The only sound was the clip-clopping of hoofs and the iron wheels of the wagon grating over the hard ground.

As they came out from the shelter of a sloping hillside, the first shot came. The bullet rapped into the wagon, as the sound echoed hard on the still air.

Brodie yelped and yanked on the reins. The wagon clattered off the road as Laredo fired at the distant burst of smoke. He spurred the horse toward the spot, levering a shell. He could see no movement. But when he reined in on a hilltop, standing in the stirrups, a second shot came, whistling near his head.

He swore and dashed down the slope toward the ambusher, his rifle ready.

But the man had gone, and there was no telling in which direction. Laredo turned back. He had come a mile or so from the wagon, and he had no doubt Brodie was trying to get away.

He saw Pete then, far to the north, moving toward the road. He met the other as he came around a low hill. Pete said he hadn't seen the shooter.

"I figger he knows this country. There must be places to hide in. . . . Where's Brodie?"

"I left him in the wagon. He's probably making his getaway. . . ."

150

Pete chuckled. "Let's go round him up."

Brodie had gone back the way they'd come, probably trying to reach the woods, but he had no chance. They came up on him from two sides and he gave up, reining in.

Laredo said, "Turn the wagon around, *amigo*."

Brodie shouted at them, "You got no right to hold me!"

Pete pulled his pistol and cocked it. "Turn the wagon around." He scowled and Laredo said loudly, "Don't shoot him!"

"Why not?"

"He's got to stand trial."

"I just gave him a trial," Pete said, growling. He pointed the pistol and Brodie cowered.

Laredo said to Brodie, "I told you not to rile him! Now, turn the damned wagon around. Don't shoot, Emilio, he's gonna do as he's told."

Brodie turned the wagon in a tight circle, wide eyes on Pete, and they went back. Pete holstered the revolver as if reluctantly, still glowering at the man on the wagon seat.

Laredo said in a low voice to Brodie, "Watch yourself, friend. When he gets a burr under the saddle he's dangerous as a sidewinder."

Brodie nodded, eyeing Pete, edging away from him.

With Laredo in the lead, they went back through the hills, but their presence brought no shots. Laredo went as far as a mile ahead and Pete rode off to the side, but they saw no one.

Near dusk they came to a tiny settlement, five houses placed in no particular pattern in a flat area, with two stores and a mostly open blacksmith shop. The store was half saloon, with a short bar and two tables.

The place was called Miller Junction, according to a sign nailed to the front of the store. It was named after the store owner, Emery Miller, a friendly sort. He was a skinny, almost weedy man, with a long face made longer by a dark, untrimmed goatee.

The store was empty of shoppers when they went in, but

151

Miller assured them Saturday was a day of booming business.

Laredo described Abner Parker, but Miller had not seen him. "Ain't been but half a dozen folks in here t'day and none of 'em half as big as you."

Laredo picked out a sackful of supplies and put them in the wagon. Miller also had some newspapers for sale but none was less than two weeks old. There was no telegraph nearby.

"You got to go to Harrisburg f'that," Miller said. "It's about forty mile over west."

It was dark when they went outside. There was a sweet-running creek a quarter of a mile from the store, Miller told them. They headed that way and found a sandy spot under some willows and cottonwoods. Laredo built a fire and they ate beans and boiled coffee. It was a peaceful spot, with the water chattering over rocks. . . .

Pete had the first watch, and Laredo curled up where he could see Brodie. The prisoner had become more and more tense and snappish, unwilling to do anything he was told. Several times Pete had had to scowl and start toward him to make him obey. He was obviously deathly afraid of Pete.

But they had only a few more days on the trail and would soon be rid of the man. He would go into the hoosegow, and it would be someone else's job to prosecute him.

Laredo drifted off to a light sleep. Ever since his days at the Tanner training grounds, he had been a light sleeper . . . a selective sleeper. A crash of thunder might not waken him, but a nearly silent footfall would find him wide-awake, reaching for his pistol. Pete was the same way. It was something they had developed in that rigorous training.

Sometime before dawn, Laredo's eyes opened. He was not certain at first what had wakened him. Someone was walking—was it a horse?—not far off. His hand slid down and his fingers curled about the butt of his revolver. The footfalls were coming closer.

Then suddenly a horse was galloping, and someone shouted. At the same time shots were fired into the camp. Laredo thumbed the hammer back and fired at the vague figure on horseback. The man was galloping through the camp, firing two pistols as fast as he could thumb them.

Laredo rolled and fired again and again, conscious that Pete was also firing. The light was very poor and the horseman was gone in a moment, the dust still settling behind him. Brodie was yelling.

Laredo rose, looking for Pete. "You all right?"

Pete came from under the wagon. "Never came near ... but Brodie caught one." Pete reloaded the rifle. "The damn fool stood up soon's the shooting started."

Brodie was shot in the foot. As the shock subsided, he wailed, rocking back and forth, holding it.

Pete held him and Laredo examined the foot. The bullet had gone through, probably smashing a couple of bones. He tied it up as best he could.

"We'll have to get him to a doctor."

"Let's put 'im in the wagon."

Brodie screamed as they moved him, but they laid him in the wagon bed as gently as they could. Pete hooked up the horse and tied his own animal on behind. He climbed to the seat and, his rifle across his knees, they started out.

They went back to Miller's store. There was no doc closer than Harrisburg, he told them. "But the road ain't bad. We had 'er dragged only a month ago."

It was a forty-mile journey. They bought a bottle of whiskey for Brodie, and he drank half of it in the first few miles.

When they stopped for a moment, Laredo tied his horse on behind the wagon. He sat beside Pete and they went on.

"Who was that shooting at us?"

Pete had gotten a better look at the horseman. "Think it was that big one, Parker. But he came and went awful fast."

"It was a damn fool stunt. . . ."

"Maybe. He figured to cut down one of us at least, to

153

even the odds." Pete rolled a cigarette. "He did us some hurt, *amigo*."

"Yes, making us go out of our way with Brodie. That gives him another chance at us."

"And at the box."

Chapter Eighteen

Turk Jessop was far down the road to San Francisco—
and had come across nobody who had seen a man hauling a
steel box. In the town of Selden, he sat in a saloon, wondering if he was chasing a rainbow.

At the next table a man was reading a newspaper, and
when he got up, he left the paper behind. Jessop retrieved
it and began to read, sipping his beer.

On page three was an item about two government agents
who had arrested a man named Jack Brodie after finding
him with a steel safe he could not explain. The man was in
jail in Loganville.

Jessop sat up. A steel safe!

How many steel safes could there be in this lonely country? He gulped the beer, staring at the paper. The man was
in jail in Loganville!

He got up and asked the bartender, "Where's Loganville?"

The man rubbed his throat. "I'd say maybe twenty mile

east and about fifteen south. You got to go to Canton first. Take the road outa town. . . ." He pointed.

"Thanks." Jessop went out and climbed on his horse.

It was nightfall when he finally reached Loganville. It was a small town scattered over the slope of a gentle hill. The jail was fieldstone and cement and looked solid as the hill it sat on.

In one of the few saloons he learned that the only law in town was a deputy named Will Tretta. Will lived in a shack behind the jail, a bartender said.

Jessop put up at the hotel and in the morning went to the jail and said hello to Tretta.

"Wondering if you got a friend of mine in the jail."

"Ain't got anybody in the jail." Tretta said.

"Nobody?"

Tretta smiled. "We got a drunk now'n then, but nobody at the moment."

Jessop shrugged. "Heard you had a feller with a safe." He smiled. "It was in the paper."

"Oh, they come and took him away days ago."

"Where'd they take 'im?"

"Carson City they said. Name was Brodie. You a friend of his?"

Jessop shook his head. "Nope, just read about it in the paper." He waved and went out to his horse.

Carson City. That was where the damn box had started out. He stopped at a store and bought supplies, tied a sack on behind the cantle, and headed out of town.

The doctor at Harrisburg was an old-timer. His office was in a house near the center of town. He came out to the wagon and looked at Brodie's foot, nodded his head, and pointed. "Carry 'im in and put him on the table."

The table, very sturdy and metal-topped, was in the office. The doctor, whose name was Shipley, laid a blanket over it and they eased him down. Brodie was completely

156

out, drunk as he would ever be. When they carried him in, the room immediately began to smell of whiskey.

"Just as well," Shipley said. "You gents wait outside, please."

The doctor's wife came in as they filed out and closed the door.

It took an hour to operate and bandage Brodie, and when they went in he looked pale as paper and was moaning slightly.

"He's still drunk," Dr. Shipley said. "My advice is to keep him that way for a while. He'll be easier to handle. Are you going far?"

Laredo nodded. "We'll do what we can."

Pete asked, "Will he be able to walk again?"

"Oh yes, but he'll limp badly, I'm afraid. That can't be helped."

"What do we owe you?"

"I'm going to have to charge you five dollars. It was a particularly difficult operation, you know."

Laredo paid him, then they carried Brodie out and laid him in the wagon bed, with the wounded foot on a wadded-up blanket to ease the jolting.

He continued to moan as they drove away.

They halted after several hours and gave Brodie another large gulp of whiskey. When they halted for the night, they left him in the wagon. He was too drunk to eat anything.

"He's lucky he only got it in the foot," Pete said, "the way he stood up. Nobody can shoot straight from a galloping horse, or he'd be dead now."

The road they were on was only a trail, used mostly by locals. The main road north, or one of them, was a day's ride to the west—or they could go back to Miller Junction, which was farther. They chose to go west.

The night was uneventful, except that Brodie sobered a bit and began to complain loudly about his foot. Pete insisted he drink more whiskey.

In the middle of the morning they were driven off the

trail by rifle shots that seemed to be aimed at the harnessed horse. The shots came from several hundred yards away on rising ground.

Laredo and Pete separated and galloped that way, but the sniper hadn't waited for them.

"He's trying to cut us down to his size," Laredo said.

Three bullets had hit the wagon, one splintering the back of the seat. Brodie was untouched, which was remarkable.

"The damn fool is luckier than he deserves," Pete said.

In the afternoon Pete drove the wagon and Laredo ranged out to the sides, investigating likely spots that a sniper might choose. He saw a horseman far in the distance as he came along a low ridge, but the man quickly disappeared.

Toward evening they came across a telegraph line that ran north and south. The poles marched across country in company with a two-track path doubtless used by repairmen.

"Why not follow it?" Pete suggested.

"It'll be rough on Brodie. . . ."

"He shouldn't have stolen the box."

"You have a way with logic."

Pete nodded and turned the horse. The repair road was much rougher than the one they had left behind, but it was certainly a more direct way to the next town with a telegraph office.

They neither saw nor heard more from the sniper the rest of the day; perhaps their having turned off on the repair road had confused him.

By nightfall Brodie was awake and reasonably sober, refusing more whiskey. His stomach was growling and he was ravenously hungry. He was surprised to see his foot professionally bandaged and had no recollection of the doctor. However, the wound hurt a great deal, he told them. "When can I walk on it?"

Laredo shrugged. "Soon's you can bear your weight."

158

They made camp in an arroyo and treated themselves to a tiny fire.

In the morning, at first light, the sniper struck again. Two rifle shots came from a distance, rapping into the wagon. Instantly Brodie sat up, staring in the direction of the sniper. Pete yelled at him to get down, but the third shot twisted Brodie and flung him back.

When Laredo reached him, Brodie was dead.

Neither of their horses was saddled; Pete returned the fire, but no more shots came.

"The damn fool stands up every time somebody fires a gun," Pete said in disgust. "I'm surprised he lived so long."

Laredo sighed. "Now I suppose we'll never learn what happened to Cutler."

They saddled the horses. Pete rode in the direction the shots had come from, the rifle butt on his thigh, but saw no one.

They wrapped the body in the blanket, but there was no shovel in the wagon. They would take the dead man to the next town and give him a decent burial. The steel box had claimed one more life.

It began to cloud up as they journeyed, and by the time they reached the town it had begun to rain. The town was Yeagar, named after its oldest inhabitant. They drove at once to the undertaking parlor and carried the now very rigid body inside.

The undertaker called himself Dr. Decker. He quickly undressed Brodie's body and studied the wound, then looked at them.

"You shoot him?"

"No. It was a bushwhacker." Laredo showed his credentials and the other looked impressed.

"The government paying for this?"

"No, we'll pay. Give him a plain pine box."

Decker looked disappointed. "Man deserves the best, you know, on his last long journey."

159

"Not this one," Pete said. "Give him the cheapest box you've got."

Decker sighed. "Very well, gentlemen. What was his name?"

"Jack Brodie . . . and that's all we know about him. He was about thirty-five, wouldn't you say?"

Decker cocked his head. "Maybe thirty-eight. But we'll clean him up a little." He wrote the name in a book. "The burying will be day after tomorrow. You going to be there?"

"No."

"I see." Decker looked at them quizzically. "I'm surprised you brought him in."

Pete said shortly, "We wouldn't have, if we'd had a shovel."

They paid for the burial and went out to the wagon. Yeagar was a small town, straggling along a single street, with a dozen saloons and several dance halls. They found the telegraph office wedged in between a harness shop and a milliner's, and sent a wire to John Fleming telling him what had transpired since their last wire. They were on their way to Carson City with the shipment box.

Fleming replied at once. He was relieved they had the box and hoped they would have no further trouble.

The rain was heavy when they came out of the telegraph office. They drove to the nearest livery and rented stalls. The stable owner was happy to let them stay the night with the wagon.

"You got money in it, friend?"

"We're delivering land grant forms to the capital."

The owner made a face and left them alone.

The storm grew worse during the night, but slackened as dawn came creeping in like a whipped dog. The street outside the stable was thick with mud, and the rain continued on and off, drizzly and damp.

Pete said, "I vote we lay up here. Another day won't hurt."

"I agree. Let's go get some breakfast."

160

"Leave the wagon alone?"

Laredo considered. "If one of us stays here, won't it be more suspicious?"

"Maybe so . . ."

They went across the street to a restaurant. It had a big sign, but was a tiny place of small-paned windows and a bench counter. The smell of bacon was strong. Someone in the back was singing an old song, "Stump-Tailed Dolly."

The room was half-full. They found places and ate bacon and eggs, listening to the political talk around them. Apparently the town was voting very soon on a mayor.

As they stepped outside the door, Laredo halted abruptly. Far down the street a big man on a light sorrel horse had just entered town. He hissed at Pete.

Pete said, "He's the one. . . ."

They had both turned toward the horseman, and he apparently saw the movement. He stared for a moment, then turned the horse and galloped away. He was too far for a revolver shot.

Laredo swore. This was the second time they'd seen the man and not been able to chase him.

Pete said, "Now he knows where we are. I'll bet he lost us in the storm. It wiped out our tracks."

Laredo grunted in disgust. "Well, he'll have plain tracks to follow now. The mud will see to that. We might as well send him a letter."

He looked at the sky. Gray and overcast, but the rain had let up. They hooked up the horse to the wagon, put feed in the wagon bed, and started out with Laredo driving and Pete loping ahead, the Winchester across his thighs.

Before midday they met a wagon train coming south and paused to exchange news—and observations. No one had seen the man on the light sorrel horse. He was probably not ahead of them.

The country was half desert and uninhabited. There was a stage station by a dry stream bed; they came on it just before dark and got down in front of the door. They could bed down in the stable, the manager said. The stage was

161

due later that night and all the cubicles were for the passengers.

The station had a kitchen and a tiny bar. They had a good meal and bitter coffee, then drifted back to the stable.

Pete said, "Why not put the steel box on the stage when it gets here?"

"And call attention to it?"

"We could go along with the stage. . . ."

Laredo shook his head. "It might be a mistake. Stages get robbed every day. They're an obvious target."

"Well, it was an idea."

Chapter Nineteen

ABNER Parker was used to getting what he wanted. As a big man, bigger than most, and good with a gun, he usually did. So he felt frustrated at not being able to whittle down the pair of government agents who had the steel box Fritz Benner was paying him well to get.

True, he had respect for them, and so did not intend to ride in shooting. He had galloped into their camp at dawn, hoping to catch them napping, but he had not. His horse had been hit twice and he'd had to get another, but he'd been lucky.

He had been surprised to see them in Yeagar. He'd lost them in the storm, but his luck was holding. It wasn't much of a town; he stationed himself on a high point where he could see the road leading in and the one leading out.

He expected them to head north, and he was not disappointed. They left early in the morning and he followed in no hurry, watching from a long distance as they stopped to gossip with members of a wagon train.

The country did not allow him to get close for the remainder of the day, and at night they stopped at a stage station.

Parker waited a mile away till it was dark, then rode in slowly and left his horse beyond the corrals. He walked in closer, to the row of cubicles for passenger use. They were tiny rooms, seven in the row, cot and mirror and nothing else—he had stayed in others like them often enough.

But as he frowned at them, he was frustrated again. Which ones held the two men? If he started opening doors, all hell might break loose. And he might get shot. People tended to be touchy about others bursting in on them in the late night.

But the wagon must be in one of the stables; he did not see it in the yard. There were two stables one beside the other, with large corrals behind them. Each had two wide doors; one was closed, the other standing open.

He paused beside the open door, and could see a wagon inside. If it was the wagon with the steel box, how could he manage to get it out? If he had a pack tree on a mule, he might be able to . . . but he didn't. There was no way he could hitch up a horse and drive the wagon away—everyone in the stage station would hear him.

It was frustrating to be so close to the box and not be able to do anything about it.

But he ought to make sure it *was* the box.

He stepped inside the stable and heard a hammer being drawn back on a pistol. A voice said, "That's far enough, friend."

Parker could see the vague shape of a man standing by the front of the wagon. He half turned and pulled his Colt at the same time, the movement hidden by his body. But as he leveled the weapon, the other fired.

Parker dropped down instantly and fired back. The other's bullet had come uncomfortably close, and had probably missed only because he had been moving. He crawled toward the open door, firing twice under the wagon. He could hear yells from the station building as he slid around the corner out of the line of fire, gained his feet, and ran around past the corrals to his horse.

As he mounted and swung the horse's head away from the station, someone began firing at him with a rifle, the slugs coming much too close. He must be a very poor target, but the man with the rifle was a good guesser.

In a few moments he was out of range, and there was no pursuit.

Parker reined in to a walk, breathing hard. That had been a very close one. Luck was still with him. Except that he had almost had his hand on the box! Almost.

And he was positive now that the only way he would come into possession of the box was to kill the two agents. They were too wary and alert.

But time was running out. He had to do it soon or they would deliver the box, and then he might have no chance at it again.

Pete was certain it had been Parker in the stable. It had been his watch, and Pete had seen the shadowy figure cross the dark yard from the station building. At first he had supposed it might be the station manager taking a last look around. He knew the man was up, expecting the evening stagecoach.

Pete had challenged the man who had entered the stable, but had not expected a shot. He slipped to the side, firing back, knowing he had missed. It must be Parker!

The intruder got away, running past the corrals. Pete followed with the rifle, firing half a dozen shots into the gloom.

The fracas roused the station, but no harm had been done; no one had been hit. The manager explained that they had occasionally been plagued by drifters who tried to steal a horse or two, and this was probably one of them. Laredo let him think so.

The stagecoach was long overdue. Laredo and Pete curled up in the stable under the wagon. In the morning the stage had still not appeared and the station keeper was very worried. There was no telegraph to tell him what had happened.

When Laredo settled up their bill the manager said, "It happens now and then—could be one of a hundred things. They's some bridges goes out damn near ever' spring. Could be one of them. But it'll be along."

"Good luck."

They drove north with Pete on the wagon seat.

It rained that day, starting in the early afternoon. They had seen no evidences of Parker. If he was following them he was staying on the horizon. They had to cross low rocky hills and go around others, but always with one of them scouting ahead.

Several times, when Laredo was riding ahead of the wagon, he glimpsed a distant horseman, but could not close with him. And several times rifle shots came at them, but always from too far away to be accurate. It was as if Parker was venting his annoyance.

The road they were on joined another more traveled road, and in a few hours they passed a stagecoach hustling in the opposite direction. Carson City was not far off.

Abner Parker gave up the chase a day outside of Carson City and rode in to report to Fritz Benner. Benner was ensconced in the Grover Hotel, and not at all happy to learn that Abner had not separated the government agents from the box.

"It ain't that easy," Parker said.

"They're only men like anybody else!"

"No they ain't. If they were ordinary men I'd have the damn box by now. They damn near killed me twice. The last week I ain't been able to get near 'em."

"They have to sleep at night. . . ."

"I don't think they ever sleep. Leastways, one of 'em's always awake."

Benner growled and paced the room. He had to have that box! Ever since that stupid little government clerk in

Washington City had told him about it, he had dreamed of its millions. How could it be so impossible?

"Where will they take the box?"

Parker made a face. "There's a Treasury agent in town. Maybe he's got a safe."

"See what you can find out about it."

"All right."

Benner continued the pacing. What were they likely to do with the box? Take it to Washington City, probably. And very likely by train. He tapped his chin, staring out the window at nothing. It would be valuable to know more about how such a box might be shipped on a train. He ought to be able to buy that information from some railroad employee who wanted to augment his income.

He asked Parker to find him such a man and Parker nodded.

He asked the big man, "Do they know you by sight?"

"Yes. I was close to 'em as I am to you now. But I didn't know who they was then."

Benner nodded and dismissed Parker. He shrugged into a coat, put on his hat, and walked to the railroad station to look at trains. It had to be possible to get at the box— maybe while the train was in motion—and toss the box off. He wished he knew more about train robbers. If only he could find and employ one . . . but of course that was probably impossible. How would one advertise for such a man?

He walked back to the hotel deep in thought—thoughts about millions of dollars.

Parker returned after dark to say he had been able to find out very little about the Treasury agent, Reinhardt. The man had an office on the main drag and there were apparently several other armed agents with him. Parker did not want to ask too many pointed questions about them.

But he had found a railroad employee who would tell them what they wanted to know. "Where you want to see him?"

"Don't bring him here. . . ." Benner considered.

"There's some barns about a block over. Nobody's using them. You could meet us there."

Benner nodded, pulling out his watch. "In an hour."

Parker left and Benner examined his pistol; he wore it in a shoulder holster. It was fully loaded. He anticipated no problems, but one should be ready. . . .

He walked to the deserted barns and found Parker waiting for him, leaning against one of the open doors. Parker said, "I got him inside. I promised him twenty-five dollars. That all right?"

"If his information is any good." Benner followed Parker into the dark interior and Parker showed him a lantern. He had examined the barn earlier, he said, and made sure it was vacant of ears.

The railroad man was a short, wizened fellow with a long-billed cap and dirty overalls. It was difficult to tell his age in the dark, but his voice sounded middle-aged.

Parker did not introduce Benner. He said, "This's Fred. Fred, you tell this gentleman what you told me."

"Where's my money?"

"You'll get your money," Benner said testily. "What I want to know is how a safe, for instance, would be transported from Carson City to Washington."

"In the baggage car."

"With guards in the car?"

Fred made a grunting noise. "D'pends on how the customer wants it."

"If the customer is the Treasury agent here?"

"It'd go with a guard or two. That's regulations."

"How would the safe get on the baggage car?"

"You bring it to the freight office, fill out the papers, and we put it on the baggage car."

"How many baggage cars are there?"

"D'pends on the amount of baggage. These days, usually one car."

"Where do the guards stay?"

"Right there in the car. They locks themselves in. Course they takes turns goin' to eat, lessen they brings

168

food with 'em. And they takes turns goin' to the lavatory."

"Does the railroad hire the guards?"

"No. Not usually."

Benner said, "When the train is going across country, does the train pick up other baggage at stops?"

"Course it does."

"I see. Other goods that would go into the baggage car."

"Yes."

"But there are guards inside. What's the signal for them to open the car?"

Fred chuckled. "I dunno. It changes alla time. There's no fixed signal."

"Ummm. All right, Fred..." Benner stepped away, nudging Parker. "Strike a match, Ab."

Parker scratched a match and Benner selected several bills. "Give these to Fred." He walked out.

Laredo and Pete waited outside of town until dark. Then they entered it slowly and went at once to Reinhardt's house and woke him up.

He was delighted to see them. "You have the box?"

"It's in the wagon. Where d'you want it?"

"Let me get dressed."

Reinhardt went with them to the office. They carried the heavy box upstairs and put it in the large safe. And when that was done, Reinhardt took a bottle from a cabinet and laid out three glasses. "This calls for a celebration." He poured into the glasses, handing them around. "Let's hope this is the end of it." He drank. "I'll get the damned box on the train soon's possible—will you go with it?"

"We're ordered to."

Pete asked, "What about Gerard Quinlan?"

"He's on his way here from Washington. I'm surprised he's not here already. Maybe he stopped off somewhere. But let's not worry about him. As far as I'm concerned the sonofabitch is a no-good, and I know for certain John Fleming thinks the same."

"Then let's all get some sleep," Laredo suggested. "When's the next train?"

Reinhardt looked at the schedule. "There's one day after tomorrow. I'll wire Fleming in the morning that the shipment box is in our hands and ready to be put on the train."

Laredo finished the drink. "Then I vote for bed."

One of Reinhardt's "sources" came to him the next afternoon with the information that Turk Jessop had been seen in the town that same day.

Reinhardt immediately informed Laredo and Pete Torres to be on the lookout. Jessop would undoubtedly try for the box.

Laredo asked, "Is he alone?"

"I don't know but my source would have told me if he'd been with someone else."

Pete said, "What happened to Shorty and Frank Slater?"

"They may turn up," Reinhardt replied. "So be careful."

The next day they carried the box down to the wagon and drove to the freight office with Reinhardt. He had the papers filled out, and they watched as two porters hauled the box away and loaded it into the baggage car.

Pete had gotten a food sack from the hotel cook, which they put onto the car; there was already a cot on board. They would sleep in their clothes for the long trip to Chicago.

Reinhardt said, "I'll wire Fleming to have men meet you in Chicago. You'll have to change trains."

They shook hands. Reinhardt wished them luck, and they climbed on board and locked the door behind them.

Chapter Twenty

THE railroad published its route and gave out copies at the ticket office. Fritz Benner studied a copy with Abner Parker. Where was the best place to hit the baggage car?

"Where they don't expect it," Parker said.

"Where is that?"

"At a water stop."

"What do you mean?"

Parker tapped his finger on the map. "The train has to stop to take on water every now and then—I don't know how often, but the stops are marked on the map."

"Those are different from ordinary stops?"

"Yes. The guards ought to be half-asleep, not expecting anything."

Benner rubbed his hands together. "That's exactly what we want." He found a cigar and lit it. "How about the getaway? After we take the box, where do we go?"

"We have a horse and wagon waiting. Where you want to go?"

Benner bent over the map. "There'll be a fuss raised of

course, so we ought to go someplace where we can wait it out. After that, we can go anywhere."

"You got to get the damn box open too."

"Yes . . . That means a big city." He tapped the map. "I'd like to take it to Kansas City." He moved his finger along the rail route. "Have you been over this line?"

Parker nodded his head. "Once or twice. There's a couple of places would be good. . . ."

"We don't have much time. According to the schedule, the train leaves tomorrow. If they're on it with the box, we won't have time to set up anything."

"Well, we can get the box, then figure it from there. We'll need a wagon, but this country is full of wagons."

"Can you get the box alone?"

"I'll have to."

"All right. I'll leave it to you. There's a great deal of money in it for you if you bring it off." Benner blew smoke. "And not much if you don't."

Parker nodded again.

He watched from a distance as the steel shipment box was loaded aboard the baggage car. The two government agents were there, and the Treasury man, Reinhardt, as well as several railroad men, all armed. Parker stared at the battered-looking box as they heaved it up and through the doors. It was so near—and yet so far.

He saw the doors slammed and locked. Reinhardt lit a cigar, chatting with the railroad men, and after a bit the train moved out as steam shushed and bells sounded. . . .

Parker swung aboard with his bag. Where the box went, he would go.

He had dynamite in the bag.

Turk Jessop put himself up in a shack on the outskirts of town, within a stone's throw of the depot. The shipment box had to go by train, and according to the schedule tacked to the depot bulletin board, the next train was tomorrow. He walked to the depot late at night and consulted the printed form by the light of a match.

He was a block away with field glasses when the Treasury agent and two men loaded the box into the baggage car.

Then Jessop boarded the train and paid the conductor for his passage to Chicago. He sat in the last car and pulled his hat down over his eyes to wait.

The express car was not large, and it was partially filled with crates and boxes of various sizes. Someone had built a bunk bed against one wall, and there were several stools piled on it.

High up on both sides of the car were tiny slits of windows for ventilation, and there was a portholelike window in the car door that could be closed off and bolted.

Laredo said, "I think we're going to catch up on our sleep, *amigo*."

"I expect so."

They spent an hour rearranging the crates and other baggage so they could sit or lie on it, using the steel shipment box as a footstool.

When an insistent rapping came on the end door, Pete opened it with his Colt leveled. It was the conductor. He was a lean, middle-aged man wearing a black billed hat and a long coat with two rows of buttons.

The conductor said, "You two are going through to Chicago. . . ."

"Yes."

Laredo said, "We'd best decide on a code. . . ."

The conductor nodded. "I was about to suggest it." He glanced at Pete's pistol. "I don't want to get shot any more than anyone else. If I have to come back here I'll rap twice, then once, then twice again. All right?"

"Twice, once, then twice again."

"Yes. I can send a lad back here with food if you like. . . ."

"Do you do that customarily?"

The conductor nodded. "Does anyone on the train know you're here?"

Laredo shrugged. "Anyone could have seen us get on, I suppose. We have to assume someone does."

The other smiled. "And I see you're ready for them. What about the food?"

"Send it back."

"Fine." The conductor opened the door and went out.

Pete said, "If Parker's on the train will he come through that door?"

"I wouldn't if I were him."

"Neither would I, not knowing what's on the other side. So you think he'll wait till Chicago?"

Laredo grinned. "If I were in his place I'd wire ahead and have a gang meet the train."

"John Fleming's going to have a gang meet us."

"It ought to be an exciting time." Laredo scratched his chin. "If Fleming does send men, I wonder if we can turn over the box to them there. I'll be happy when we get rid of it."

"*Verdad*." Pete crossed himself. Then he sat and put his feet up on the box.

The time seemed to pass very slowly. The sounds and the motion of the train lulled them. A young black came to the door with a food tray, giving the correct knock, and Pete let him in. He waited till they ate, then took the tray and the plates back.

Laredo opened the door window and watched the scenery slide by. The sky was a deep blue, fading out near the horizon, gaining a greenish tinge that turned into milky white where it merged with distant mountains. Nothing moved out there, not even a hunting hawk. As the tracks curved, he could see the panting engine with black smoke pouring from its tall stack.

Pete slept in the bunk for several hours, then Laredo took his turn. The time crept by. When night fell they lit a lantern and hung it by a wire from the ceiling. It brought huge shadows into being as it swayed back and forth.

But the night passed, and before noon the train stopped at a depot to take on passengers. No one came near the baggage car.

Half a mile from the depot the train stopped again to take on water. Laredo opened the car door to watch this process, and to air out the car. Two or three men stepped off the cars ahead but they stayed near the iron steps.

Laredo watched them closely, but none seemed familiar. Maybe Parker was not on the train.

Pete said, "If he's not on the train, then he'll possibly meet it somewhere."

"How could he get ahead of the train?"

Pete grinned. "Couldn't he wire ahead and have someone meet it?"

Laredo rolled his eyes. "You mean he's got an organization?"

"Then he's on the train." Pete sighed. "Waiting for his Chicago gang—the one you gave him a bit ago."

Turk Jessop sat in the last passenger car, just ahead of the baggage car. He bought a newspaper from the boy who brought a stack of them through the train at the first stop. He read it through, then slept, stared through the grimy window, and wondered how he was going to get at the steel box.

He noticed the young black with the food trays who went into the baggage car. He could easily overpower the lad and get the tray—and get into the car, he thought.

But then he'd be facing two armed and very dangerous men. He didn't care for the odds. He could not spend one thin dime of the loot if he were dead.

Each time the train stopped he watched the baggage car intently, but no one got off and no baggage was put aboard.

How was he going to get his hands on the box?

It was a long way to Washington, D.C.; maybe a chance would present itself. They would have to change trains at Chicago, of course. He would watch for an opportunity. If he could somehow grab the box, it ought to be easy to lose himself in that city.

Chapter Twenty-One

BY the time the train reached Chicago they were heartily tired of the baggage car. It was confining, too dark as a rule, dusty, and monotonous. It was like being in prison, Pete said.

And the food was barely adequate; however, its coming was one of the bright spots of the day.

But they both breathed sighs of relief when the train rolled huffing and shushing into the station at Chicago. Through their small window they watched the passengers debark, and after an interval the conductor came back to rap on their door.

He had a slim, dapper-looking man with him. "I'm Gerard Quinlan," the man said quickly. He offered a paper. "I'm ordered to take charge of the shipment box at once."

Laredo took the paper and read it, with Pete looking over his shoulder. Quinlan was right: it was an order from John Fleming's superiors. Quinlan was in charge.

He pointed to the box. "It's there."

Quinlan stared at it. "What happened to it? It's all brown."

"Somebody painted it."

Quinlan examined it. "Well, they didn't open it." He gazed at them. "Well, we won't be needing you any longer. I have my own men. They'll be along in a moment."

Laredo nodded. He and Pete got their things together and, taking their rifles, went into the next car and stepped off the train.

They watched as a small hand truck was pushed to the baggage car; the doors were opened, and Quinlan and two others lifted the box down into the truck.

Laredo said, "Well, what d'you think?"

"I think we follow the box. Do you suppose he'll lose it before he gets it to the street?"

"He might at that."

But he did not. Quinlan had planned ahead. There was a small covered wagon waiting; he and his two men lifted the box into it without incident. Then they got inside and the wagon drove off.

Laredo and Pete hailed a hack and followed.

They watched as the brown box was placed in another baggage car. Quinlan and his two men locked themselves in.

Laredo bought two tickets and they got on the train with a hundred others. The cars were crowded, and they had to settle for seats two cars away from the baggage car.

It was vastly disappointing to be unceremoniously pushed off the job before it was finished. But Quinlan had proper orders, signed by authorities, and they could hardly be argued with. John Fleming, they knew, would be as annoyed as they; his opinion of Quinlan was no higher than theirs—and they could be satisfied that Fleming had fought a good battle to keep Quinlan from returning.

But Fleming had lost. However, he had ordered them to do what they could. They would accompany the steel box, if not in the baggage car with it, then on the same train as passengers.

They would report to Fleming in Washington. Under the circumstances, it was all that was possible.

Turk Jessop, watching from a distance, had seen no possibility of getting his hands on the steel box during the move from one train to the other in Chicago. He followed along, taking advantage of crowds and cover, but there were six men around the box, not counting trainmen.

Hoping against hope, he got on the same train, but what could he do alone? He had little chance. . . . He was beginning to think his best chance had long since flown. He had been in possession of the box once, and had been double-crossed. It rankled and gnawed at him that the box had been his. He could be rich by now. It was all Frank Slater and Shorty's fault; they had ruined a sure thing. He cursed them every day of his life.

He had managed to change his appearance somewhat; he had no fear that a casual glance would expose him. He took a seat as close to the baggage car as possible. Without seeming to, he watched every person who went into the baggage car and returned, but no opportunity presented itself.

Abner Parker, now clean-shaven, wearing different clothes, with a pipe in his mouth as camouflage, watched the move calmly. The Treasury people were taking extreme precautions; even the local police were in evidence, sidling through the crowds, eyeing everyone. It would take a troop of cavalry to get the steel box away.

Parker followed sedately and boarded the train with his luggage, taking a seat where he could watch the box being loaded into the baggage car.

He had given his next move considerable thought, and would make it in about two days. He had composed and sent wires to Fritz Benner, using their simple code, telling

178

Benner to have men just north of the little town of Lenz, in Ohio, when the train came through. They must have a wagon and must take orders from him, Parker.

A confirming wire reached Parker on the train. All would be arranged as he'd said.

Shortly after the train left Chicago, Parker discussed the route with the conductor, first setting his watch with the trainman's. He asked about Lenz and learned the train would reach that town at night, as he had calculated.

The conductor studied his silver watch. "We will reach Lenz at eleven forty-two, sir."

"Thank you."

The conductor looked at him curiously. "But we don't stop there, you know."

"I know." Parker smiled. "It's only nostalgia. I used to live in that little town."

"Ahhh," the trainman said, satisfied. "I'm sorry then we don't go through in daylight. You won't be able to see a thing. . . ."

"Well—just being there." Parker shrugged. The conductor smiled and went on. He would remember the conversation, Parker thought.

The time was approaching. Parker sat in his seat, glancing at his watch every half hour, going over what he had to do in his mind. He must do it perfectly the first time . . . and time itself was important. Extremely important!

But at last it was nine o'clock and the lights in the car were dimmed. People curled up in the chair cars, the porters made up the beds in the sleepers, and people crawled in, including Parker. But he kept his clothes on.

He forced himself to lie still, the watch in his hand. Two hours crept by, the longest he had ever known. But at last it was eleven-fifteen.

He slid out of the bed, taking his small black bag, and slowly walked back to the baggage car. Most passengers were asleep behind the curtains. If anyone noticed him he would think Parker was on his way to the privy.

179

At the end of the car he waited a moment, listening. Then he opened the door and stepped onto the tiny platform between the cars. The familiar rattle and rush of the cars was more pronounced, along with the loud click-clacking of the wheels on the rails.

Opening the bag, he took out the sticks. He had his movement planned, had done this a hundred times in his head. He quickly wedged the dynamite sticks into crevices in the baggage car. Four sticks should more than do the job.

He glanced at his watch; it was time.

Striking a match, he held the flame to the fuse ends and watched them fizz. Each fuse would burn for five minutes. He paused a few seconds to make sure they were burning. There was no possibility of their being blown out by the wind.

Then he opened the door and hurried back to his berth.

Turk Jessop was surprised to see the big man go past him to the baggage car at that hour. What was up? He uncurled himself from the chair, rubbing his eyes. Was there a plot to get at the steel box? He pulled out his pistol and spun the cylinder, then shoved it back into his belt.

Was the big man in cahoots with the guards?

Jessop rose, then sat down again quickly, hearing the big man open and close the door, coming back. The man, carrying the same bag, went past him, seeming to be in a hurry. What the hell was going on? Was the big man making plans with the guards? What else could it be?

He waited a minute or two in case the man returned, but he did not. Jessop pulled out the pistol and opened the door, stepping onto the platform between the cars.

As he closed the door behind him he saw the fuse ends, saw the smoke curling—and realized in one startled instant what the man had done.

Then the world came apart.

* * *

Parker gained his berth, heart thumping. At the explosion the train would stop. He would jump off and run back to the baggage car. The hired men should be there with the wagon—two men at least if Benner was efficient. Their job was to dig the box out of the wreckage while everyone else on the train was either stunned or wondering what had happened.

He had barely crawled into his berth when the huge explosion came—and he was not prepared for the extent of it! It seemed to lift and shake the entire train with a deep, wrenching blast!

Instantly the engineer braked and women screamed. The sounds of the wheels skidding on the rails added to the din. All up and down the cars people began to shout; several women in his car kept up a high-pitched shrieking. People filled the aisles, yelling to each other.

Parker slid out and pushed his way to the nearest door as the overhead lights flickered. He opened the door and stood on the steps as the train came to a jerking halt. Jumping down in the dark, he ran back toward the baggage car—that did not exist! It was smashed into matchsticks.

He could see instantly that no one inside could have survived. Even the big wheel trucks were twisted and had been thrown off the tracks.

Where was the box?

Off to his right a lantern was swinging and a man called out his name. Parker turned, yelling at him to hurry.

"I'm Parker—how many of you?"

"Two," the man said. "We got us a wagon right here. . . ." He shouted to one of the hired men, George, to bring the wagon along. Then he hurried to the train, lifting the lantern high. "Jesus! You blew the shit out'n her!"

"Get in there and find the box," Parker ordered.

The man began to pull at the wreckage. George backed the wagon up as close to the roadbed as he could, then jumped out and ran to the wrecked car.

Parker yelled, "Hurry up! Hurry up!"

Men were getting off the train, milling about. He could

181

hear people shout that this person or that was hurt. Lanterns were lit and he could see trainmen bustling about, helping some off the cars.

A few men started toward him, and Parker pulled his pistol. He fired twice into the air and they halted and went back.

George found the box—both men muscled it out of the splintered wreck and hauled it to the wagon, dumping it in.

"Get out of here!" Parker snarled. His nerves were at a breaking point. He jumped on the wagon as George gathered up the reins and slapped them. He blew out the lantern as the other man piled in and they drove into the dark.

There was a road paralleling the tracks and George turned into it, toward the town.

Parker looked back at the people on the tracks, where lanterns were moving here and there.

He took a long breath. They had the box!

Laredo and Pete Torres were fast asleep in an upper and lower when the explosion came. Laredo sat up instantly, sure they'd had a head-on collision with another train.

His next thought was of the baggage car.

The train jerked and rumbled to a halt, throwing people out of the berths or toppling them in the aisles. People began to shout and women screamed. There was instant panic.

Pete yelled in Laredo's ear, "The baggage car!"

Laredo nodded. He took precious moments to pull on his pants and boots, then he grabbed his shirt and pistol and slid out to the aisle. Pete was there beside him, thrusting arms into shirtsleeves.

They shoved and pushed their way through a mob of dazed and frantic passengers to reach the door, hearing shots. Someone fired twice a short distance away.

Jumping to the ground, they could see a lantern moving where the baggage car should be.

The conductor yelled, "Back, everybody—don't get yourselves shot!"

Laredo ignored him and ran toward the baggage car with Pete at his heels. As they approached it the lantern went out and they could hear a wagon rattling away in the gloom.

They were too late.

The baggage car no longer existed. The explosion had completely shattered it. Laredo gritted his teeth. Quinlan and two men had been inside it. Turning, he yelled for the trainmen to bring lanterns.

Pete said, "They were after the damned box."

"And they got it, too . . . or they wouldn't have left."

Several trainmen ran up with lanterns and by their light the wreck looked even worse. A few small fires had started and they were quickly doused. At the far end of the car they found the three battered bodies; one of the trainmen covered them, saying they would bring an undertaker from town in the morning.

Part of the next passenger car was also wrecked, and several people hurt. There was no possibility of the train's moving. . . . The conductor sent a man running into town to the telegraph office.

The wreckage was strewn along the tracks for a hundred yards, and even the tracks themselves at the point of the explosion were smashed and bent.

Pete said, "Nothing we can do here. . . ."

Laredo agreed. They went back to the passenger car for their bags and rifles, then set out to follow the wagon.

It was not a dark night and the deep wheel tracks of the heavily loaded wagon were plain in the dirt. It headed for Lenz.

They had to walk a mile or so to reach the town. It was too bad about Quinlan and his men, Laredo thought, but it had been fate. If Quinlan hadn't ordered them off the baggage car. . . .

Pete was thinking the same thing. He said, "That could have been us, smashed into nothing."

"Don't think about it."

"Do you suppose it was Parker? How'd he have a wagon waiting?"

"If it was Parker, he wired ahead and arranged it. He could know when the train would reach this point—the conductor would tell him." He glanced at Pete. "You had that all figured out as I remember . . . from your old train-robbing days."

"Yes, the Torres gang was notorious."

"Where the hell are these people going with the box?"

"Into town—I suppose that's where this road goes. I wonder if Quinlan had a key to the box."

"That's a very interesting idea." Laredo scratched his jaw. "If they got it, they'll open the box as soon as they can. Then they'll get rid of the box. Not good for us."

"Not good at all."

The little town, when they entered it, was mostly dark, only a very few lights showing. The telegraph office was lit—the trainman would have reported the wreck so that another engine would not plow into the train.

The town was only a collection of buildings strung out along a long, wide, rutted street. The explosion had not wakened the town apparently.

They had lost the trail of the wagon before they reached the town, in the ruts of other wagons. Pete looked at the sky and announced it was three hours before sun-up.

"Nothing we can do until then," Laredo said. "We need horses. . . ."

If the train robbers had come here they were either in one of the buildings, or they had gone on through the town. There were wagons parked here and there, but it was impossible to tell if any one of them was the wagon that had carried the box. Laredo suggested they curl up in one of the sheds by the livery and wait for dawn.

They were hanging over the near corral, looking at the horses, when the stable owner opened his doors.

After an hour of examining horses and haggling, they

bought two horses and saddles, then had breakfast in the town's only restaurant.

The road through the town went to Denker, the restaurant owner told them, about a forty-mile ride. "They's a stageline there, goes east and west."

"Does the train stop there?"

"No, they's only the stage."

Outside on the street, Pete said, "They're going to take the stage at Denker."

"I wish we knew for certain who 'they' were."

Pete grunted. "What about the steel box? Can they put it on the stage without arousing suspicion?"

"Maybe. Some time has passed since it disappeared. People might not be looking for it—expecting it."

Pete rolled a cigarette. "And maybe they got it open."

Laredo sighed deeply. "If they did . . . we may never find it. Or Parker either. Keep your fingers crossed. . . ."

"All right. Let's go to Denker."

They bought food, put it in sacks, and set out. The journey took nearly a day and a half by the road. A steady wind blew into their faces for hours, and if a recent wagon had left tracks, they were dusted away now.

The trip was uneventful. Denker proved to be a much larger town, with a freshly painted stageline office building and a wide area of corrals with both horses and mules, and repair shops in a long line next to the corrals. As they rode in a Concord was being prepared for the western run.

They got down in front of the office and consulted a tacked-up schedule on the office wall. According to it an eastbound stage had gone out that morning, early.

Laredo went inside, showed his credentials, and the manager took him into a small, stuffy office.

"What can I do f'you?"

"We're looking for one or two men with a safe."

"A safe?"

Laredo held his arms out. "About this size, squarish, painted brown. Pretty heavy."

The manager was a stout man, red-faced and round-shouldered. He nodded quickly. "I seen something like that! They had it wrapped in what looked like an old blue army blanket. The boys put it in the boot—heavy as hell, like you say."

"How many with it?"

"Only one man. He left east this morning. Big man, a little taller'n you."

So it was Parker, Laredo thought. "Where'd he buy a ticket to?"

"I dunno. Lemme see." The manager got up and hurried out. He was back in a few minutes. "Bought a ticket for Lankersville."

"Lankersville? It sounds like a small town."

The manager smiled. "Well, the town ain't much, but it's a division point on the railroad. There's a roundhouse and you can get a train for most anywhere."

Chapter Twenty-Two

As the miles dropped away behind the wagon, Abner Parker felt better and better. They rolled through the little burg of Lenz, and were far along the road to Denker by morning.

They reached Denker in time for the stage. He paid off the two men Benner had hired, had the box, wrapped in an army blanket, put on the stage, and settled back with a great sigh as the six-horse team pulled the Concord out onto the road to Lankersville and the railroad.

He was certain he had left any pursuit far behind.

Now he had decisions. He had not wired Benner of his success. As far as he knew, Benner was on the train heading east. But what loyalty did he have toward Benner? The man had paid him—but he had worked for the money.

Most of all, since the steel box rightfully belonged to the government, did Benner have any more claim on it than he did? Of course not.

Why should he share it with Benner?

Where should he go? If Benner began to suspect—because he had not wired him—that he was going into business for himself, what would he do? Probably murder. Benner was resourceful and dangerous as hell.

He might expect Parker to go east with the box. So, at Lankersville, Parker would go west again, or maybe south. He might even go to Mexico.

But whatever he did, he had to get the damned box open. He had to get what was inside and get rid of the thing that could mark him. Benner would tell his hired thugs to get the man with the box.

It was at once a treasure and a liability.

The stagecoach took forever. It made a dozen stops, to put men off and take others on. It stopped at three little burgs along the route, and at two stage stations where food and drink were available.

At each stop Parker got out and watched the men at the boot, his hand on the butt of his pistol. But nothing untoward took place. The wrapped box was treated like any other piece of luggage. Probably the old army blanket helped.

He managed to sleep on the jouncing stagecoach; it had no springs, only leather braces, and was notoriously hard on the liver. He got an hour here and an hour there, as everyone else did, and when the road was reasonably level and graded managed to get several hours in a row.

He awoke only when people around him began to stir. The stagecoach was coming into Lankersville.

Laredo rose from the chair. "How far is Lankersville?"

"About a hundred miles—if you foller the road." The red-faced manager pointed to the large map on the wall. "But you can save twenty miles'r more if you cuts across country." He traced the route with a stubby finger. "We's here and Lankersville is right here. But the road makes a big curve because the stage serves them other towns, here, here, and here. But you can go straight across on a horse."

A hundred miles! Laredo thanked the man and hurried outside. He found Pete at a water trough with the two horses. He told the other what he'd learned.

"If we're lucky we can beat the stage there."

Pete nodded. "Then we'd better get moving."

They were in farm country, though all the land was not under cultivation, by any means. It was wild prairie, rolling and desolate between farms. Occasionally they were able to follow a rutted road, but most often they were moving across country by the aid of distant landmarks to keep them in a straight line. The way was mostly southeast.

At night they halted to build a small fire and broil strips of meat, and rest for a few hours. Then they were in the saddles again, moving steadily.

The steady pace dropped the miles behind them. And their navigation proved to be good; they only missed the towns by a few miles. They had to backtrack when they came across the railroad right of way, and followed it into town. The stage from Denker had not yet arrived.

Parker—if it was indeed Parker on the stage—would probably put up a fight when they confronted him. They got down in front of the town marshal's office to enlist his help. The marshal was an old-timer, lean and weatherbeaten, a man of probably sixty years. He looked very capable, however, and listened to them, nodding his head slowly.

"Don't want to get folks hurt," he said. "If they's a good deal of shootin' in the middle of town, somebody's gonna get plugged."

Laredo said, "There may not be any way around it."

"Will this feller give up if he sees a bunch of us?"

"I dunno," Laredo said with a shrug. "He wants that box something fierce."

"Well, we'll do what we can. The stage station is at the other end of town. We'll wait for 'em there."

Pete asked, "When is the stage due?"

"This afternoon, late." The marshal looked at his watch. "Couple of hours."

* * *

Abner Parker opened the stage door and shouted to the driver, asking him to pull up.

When the stagecoach halted, Parker jumped down. "Much obliged." He pulled the blanket-wrapped box out of the boot onto the dusty road and waved to the driver. The coach moved on.

He was on the outskirts of town. Half a dozen sheds and falling-down shacks were in a field to his right. Someone had a fire going in front of one. To his left, maybe two hundred yards away, was a house with a picket fence around it. There were two buckboards parked just inside the fence.

Parker heaved the heavy box into the tall weeds alongside the road. When he stepped away from it, the box was well enough hidden. No one would see it unless he came very close.

He walked along the road to the house and paused by the fence. He had thought to ask if he could rent one of the wagons. He pulled out his money. He had less than twenty dollars left. Not enough to rent a horse and wagon and buy a railroad ticket too. He swore and went on down the road toward town. He'd have to think of something. . . .

The marshal had two deputies and called them both in, explaining what they had in mind to do. They would confront Parker when he got off the stage. With five guns on him Parker should give up. Any logical mind would.

The stage depot was good-sized: a large waiting room with a huge bellied stove in the center, a long, porchlike front with two doors, and a wide yard where another Concord was parked. To the rear were shops and corrals. The stage would pull up in front of the waiting room, the marshal told them, to unload passengers and baggage. Then it would roll into the yard.

His plan was to surround the stage as soon as it stopped. Parker would be a fool to attempt to shoot his way out.

Laredo and Pete agreed to the plan, examined their weapons—and waited. The stage was late, but that was not unusual. Any storm in the hills could slow it by causing washouts.

But it appeared at last, the six horses seeming to know there were corn and oats to be had in moments. When the coach halted in front of the waiting room, all five of them surrounded it with drawn revolvers.

But Parker was not on the stage.

The surprised driver said, "A feller got off t'other end of town. . . ."

Laredo blew out his breath. "He outfoxed us."

He and Pete ran for their horses. They galloped to the far end of town but saw no one who looked like Parker.

Pete said as they drew up, "Maybe someone met him."

Laredo nodded. It was likely. "At least we know he's in this town—with the box."

"He may be looking at us this minute. . . ."

Laredo searched the near buildings with his eyes. "He couldn't have had more than fifteen minutes to get off the stage and do something with the box—it's probably sitting in some wagon close by right this minute."

Pete said, "We can't search the entire town. . . ."

"I think you're right. Someone met him." He looked at the sky. "It'll be dark in an hour, dammit."

Pete peered down the road, the way the stage had come. "Do you suppose he went back?"

Laredo turned. "That's a good possibility—let's go."

They galloped out of town, following the stage road. In several miles they came to a rise and reined in. They could see four or five miles farther on; the road went straight as a rail, losing itself in the misty distance. There was no wagon on the road.

"He didn't come back," Pete said. "And I didn't see a turnoff. . . ."

"That means he's still in the town."

They rode back slowly, watching the sides of the road for wheel marks and seeing none. It was dark when they reentered the town.

They had another discussion with the marshal. He took

down a description of Parker and promised to have his men make the rounds of hotels and boarding houses.

"He's dangerous as hell, Marshal," Laredo said. "Tell them to be very careful."

The marshal said, "He's in this town to get the train, isn't he? We can keep him from gettin' on it—with a little luck."

"Why do you say 'luck'?"

"Because they's a lot of baggage goes on the train from here. If he's got somebody workin' with him we might have trouble."

"The box could be put into a larger crate," Pete observed. "We wouldn't recognize it."

"Damn!" Laredo said, annoyed. "That's exactly what he'll do!"

The marshal said, "But he'll get on the train too. . . ."

"Not necessarily. He could consign the box somewhere and go after it months from now."

Pete shook his head and looked at Laredo. "Troubles, *amigo.*"

Chapter Twenty-Three

LANKERSVILLE was a town of several thousand souls; it was a railroad town, existing only because it was a division point and had a large and busy roundhouse half a mile from the outskirts.

Abner Parker stole a railroad man's billed cap in a saloon and got a room in a boardinghouse, telling the woman owner that he was a roundhouse worker temporarily laid off. It was the kind of story she had heard a hundred times and she gave it not another thought, since he paid the rent a week in advance.

When the marshal's deputy came round asking questions, she told him she had no strangers, only railroad men.

Each night Parker walked to the end of town to make sure the box was still there. He pulled it down into the ditch and covered it with weeds so someone would have to stumble over it to discover it.

How would he get it on the train?

He knew a search for him and the box was going on, and that they probably had a good description of him. But he had changed his appearance, and was wearing the billed cap; of course his height was against him, but there were other tall men. . . .

If he could get his hands on a wagon, he could hit the trail for the next train stop and put the box on there. But he would have to buy a wagon and horse, or steal them.

Stealing a horse was not good. People got very exercised about it. He ought to buy the horse and steal just the wagon. But he needed money badly. After paying for the room and buying food, he had very little left.

But he had his pistol.

He quickly learned when the railroad payday was, a Friday. Men gathered in the saloons, buying each other drinks, singing, telling stories, having a good time, and getting drunk.

Late Friday night, Parker waited outside a saloon and followed three men in turn, confronting each with a cocked pistol, taking money from each.

When he returned to his rented room he had forty-seven dollars in cash. Not as much as he'd wanted, but better than nothing. But still not enough to buy a horse.

And the next railroad payday was two weeks away.

How was he going to get the damned box out of town?

Laredo wired John Fleming at once, telling him where they were and that they were reasonably sure the man who had stolen the box, Parker, was still in Lankersville with it. Fleming had heard about the dynamiting of the baggage car and the deaths of Gerard Quinlan and the two agents. He assured them they were again in charge. It was too bad about Quinlan. He asked them if they needed assistance, and Laredo wired back that he thought they would be able to handle it.

A number of trains had passed through the town, and Pete and Laredo had investigated each baggage car with the marshal standing by. They did not find the steel box.

The marshal's search of hotels and boardinghouses had also turned up nothing. Parker had to be somewhere—but

194

where? Did he know someone in town? That was the next possibility. But it was very little help.

Pete said, "Maybe he's *not* in town."

"Then where did he go—with the box?"

"To the next train stop. That's what I'd do."

Laredo frowned. A very good suggestion. He asked the marshal, "How far is the next stop?"

The old-timer looked on the map. "'Bout a hunnerd and fifty miles, I'd say . . . as the crow flies."

"A long wagon trip," Pete said, rolling a cigarette. "I'd think twice about it."

"Why does he have to take the box?" the marshal asked, puzzled.

Pete grinned. "Because he can't get it open. He has to take it somewhere he can find a locksmith with the ability to open it. It's a very special lock."

"The damn gover'ment's gettin' smart."

"In this case."

That night as they sat in a saloon over beers, Laredo said, "You could be right—he's not in this town at all. We could be wasting our time while he's getting away."

"All right, but how did he do it? How did he get the box out of town? He certainly couldn't carry it. He *had* to have a wagon or a cart at least. There hasn't been one reported stolen. Did he buy a horse and wagon?"

"You sure ask a lot of questions."

Pete sipped the beer. "There have been some robberies lately, according to the marshal. Was it Parker?"

"You mean he needed money?"

"It's a guess."

Laredo nodded. "Money to buy a horse and wagon. Are we saying he's given up the idea of putting it on a train?"

"Maybe he knows how closely we're watching the trains."

"You suggested he'd put it in a larger crate. . . ."

"Yes, if he had a carpenter shop handy." Pete got out the makin's. "We can ask around."

"You think he's still in town then?"

Pete nodded. "I do."

Laredo agreed. "I do too."

Parker slept in the daytime most days, and prowled the town at night. He located half a dozen wagons, any one of which would do fine. There were a hundred corrals in town and on the outskirts, with both mules and horses. It might be wise to steal a mule instead of a horse. . . .

He always paid his rent promptly, so Mrs. Browder would not gossip about him. He saw her infrequently and when he did, never failed to tell her that he had been talking with his foreman, who told him he would soon be back on the job. That reassured her and bolstered his story.

He had about given up the idea of putting the box on the train. The baggage cars were so closely watched—he had seen the marshal and the two government men looking through them. He would be foolish to attempt it. There was far too much at stake.

He had forgotten Fritz Benner till one morning he happened to be awake, reading a newspaper in the parlor, when a man came to the door and asked Mrs. Browder if she had a boarder named Parker. Browder of course said she had not and after a few more questions the man went away. Parker jumped up and stared at him through the window. The man looked like a thug, and was not one of the marshal's deputies.

He thought of Benner instantly.

Benner was scouring the land for him!

It was time to get the hell out! Everything was stacked against him. He had almost no money left; soon he'd have to make more six-gun withdrawals, and that was always chancy. He might easily be shot by the man he was holding up.

It was a long way to the next train stop, a damned long way to carry the precious box, but there seemed to be no other door open to him.

He managed to get a sackful of canned goods and then, selecting a night, he went hunting for a mule and wagon.

Laredo and Pete had both taken to accompanying the marshal on his nightly rounds. They were convinced that if Parker did attempt to haul the steel box out of town he would do it at night.

There was no wagon traffic at night; people hauled their goods in daylight. There were no street lamps or lights on the roads—and who was in that big a hurry?

So when Laredo noticed a man hitching up a mule to a wagon late at night, he paused. The man was tall and wore a trainman's cap. Could this be Parker?

The man had noticed him because of the sounds of his horse's footfalls. It was very quiet in the town. The man stopped working with the mule, and for several minutes made no movement at all. It was dark, but Laredo thought he was backing away.

Laredo moved toward the wagon slowly.

He had almost reached the wagon when the man fired at him. Three shots came close together—and one clipped his hat brim!

Laredo slid off the horse, pulling his pistol. This must be Parker!

He heard rapid footfalls as the man ran directly away from him. Laredo followed, thinking Parker must be desperate and possibly not thinking well. The shots would bring Pete and the marshal. Certainly not what Parker wanted. Maybe there was frustration there as well.

He caught glimpses of the running man but did not fire. The light was miserable for shooting. He tried to keep him in view but followed mostly by sounds.

Parker ran through to another street, crossed it, and disappeared between two buildings. The man might well know the town better than he did, Laredo thought.

He went between the buildings, wary of an ambush, and came out behind a row of stores. Pausing to listen, he heard nothing. Before him there were a hundred places to hide. And to flush an armed man out at night would be very dangerous.

Raising the pistol he fired into the air twice, and reloaded. That ought to bring Pete.

It did. Pete came like a shadow, on foot, calling his name softly. Laredo answered and told the other what had happened. "He's here somewhere. . . ."

Pete grinned in the gloom. "But he can't wait for morning."

"That's right. He's got to get away to wherever he hides before the light shows him."

They walked the length of the stores, moving very slowly, a dozen feet apart, and saw no one. There were sheds and privies and piled-up debris waiting to be burned, and a man could find a nest in or behind any of it.

Laredo stopped by a pile of wood and paper, then felt for a match. He struck it and put it into the pile. In a moment the flame danced up and he moved away quickly. In another minute the pile was a pyre, burning fiercely, lighting the entire area.

But the light did not reveal Parker.

Had he outdistanced them, been quicker than he'd thought? Laredo doubted it—but where was he?

The blaze created vast shadows that moved as the flames danced. Several times Laredo was on the point of firing, then realized it was only a shadow.

Very cautiously they investigated every hiding place without finding the hidden man. And the fire began to die.

Then there was a shot—and another, from the street in front of the row of stores. Someone shouted. Laredo motioned to Pete. "He must have climbed to the roofs!"

They ran around the end of the buildings and met the marshal. He had fired at a fleeing man, he said. "A big, tall man!"

Chapter Twenty-Four

"**I**T was Parker," Pete said. "Did you hit him?"

The marshal shook his head. "I don't know. Too goddam dark." He pointed to a building with a big sign: LAND OFFICE. "He come around that sign there and clumb down to the street. I was halfway up the block when I seen him. I yelled and he fired at me and ran across the street there." He indicated a vacant lot.

They went across the lot slowly and gained the next street, which was only a lane. To the right were houses, and they turned that way.

Had Parker been on the verge of getting out? If not, why was he hitching up the mule this late at night?

But Laredo had looked into the wagon as he passed. The steel box had not been in it. That was a run of bad luck—if they had spotted Parker and followed him, he might have led them to the box.

At the end of the street they halted. Parker had gone to ground somewhere—and there were plenty of places.

"No tellin' where he went." The marshal sounded disgusted.

Laredo looked at the row of houses. There were six on the street and one was a boardinghouse, according to the sign on a fence: MRS. BROWDER'S ROOMS.

Pete saw him looking at it. "Yeh—he could be in there."

All the windows were curtained. Parker could be standing behind them, staring at the three of them in the street. Laredo motioned and they moved away. Going into a house like that after a man could be explosive. One never knew what he might be up against. It would be much smarter to wait until Parker came out. That meant a vigil. . . .

Pete was reading his thoughts. "We can watch the front and back doors. . . ."

The marshal frowned. "What if he didn' go in there?"

"Hunch," Laredo said. "I've got a feeling he did. What you figure, *amigo*?"

Pete nodded. "I've got the same hunch."

The stable in the rear of the house was large, with six stalls, five of them occupied, with saddles and harnesses hung on one wall. There was also a small black buggy that probably belonged to Mrs. Browder.

They matched cartridges to decide who stayed where, and Laredo won the stable. Pete had been gone only a minute when the back door of the house opened and Parker came out.

He was carrying a rifle, and as he came through the door he levered it and let the hammer down.

Halfway down the steps he saw Laredo. Laredo stood in the doorway of the stable, twenty feet away. "You're under arrest, Parker."

Parker's reaction was instant. The muzzle of the rifle came down and he fired, jumping back at the same time. The bullet smashed the wood panel over Laredo's head.

Pulling his pistol, Laredo fired at the man, who disappeared into the house. He ran to the steps, firing again. When he opened the door Parker fired, shattering the latch.

Laredo went to his knees, then flung himself prone. He could see the murky shadow in the hall, partially silhouetted against the glass of the front door. He fired again and heard Parker cough.

In a moment the other slumped, and Laredo heard the clatter as the Winchester hit the hard floor.

The house was aroused, with voices calling out, then someone came down the stairs haltingly and a woman's voice said, "What's doing there?"

By the mealy lantern light, Laredo could see Parker slumped, facedown on the floor. He got up and walked to the body, feeling for a pulse. There was none.

Pete was at the front door, pounding furiously. Laredo went past the woman with the lantern and let him in.

Pete's pistol was cocked, and he put it away slowly as he saw Laredo. Then he looked beyond, into the hall, and sighed, seeing Parker's body.

But where was the steel box?

The next morning they searched Parker's room and found nothing. A careful search of the stable turned up nothing of interest to them.

They questioned Mrs. Browder, a stout widow woman who told them Parker had brought nothing into the house but a small bag. She was astounded that he hadn't been a railroad man at all.

At the telegraph office they wired John Fleming to say they had finished the man who'd stolen the box, but it was still unfound. Fleming's wire was curt: Find it.

In the saloon next door to the marshal's office, they sat at a small table with steins of beer before them. Pete said, "The last time anybody saw the box it was on the stage-coach."

"And the driver said he'd let Parker off outside of town and Parker had pulled the box out of the boot."

"So Parker is standing in the road with the box. Did somebody meet him there?"

"How could anyone meet him? Unless that someone was willing to wait hours and hours. The stage schedule could easily be off a full day."

"That's true. So we're back to Parker standing in the road with the box. What did he do?"

"What if he hid the box?"

Pete made a face and rolled a brown cigarette. "Where, in the ditch?"

"Maybe. Who expects to find a couple million dollars in a ditch?"

"Let's go ask the stage driver where he let Parker off."

Laredo nodded. "Good idea."

But the driver was out on a run and would not be back into town for another day or two, depending on the roads, a clerk told them.

Laredo said, "Let's go look at the ditches along the road."

They spent an hour walking along the ditch, starting from the edge of town, walking for a mile or so on both sides of the road . . . and found nothing.

Pete said, "He didn't hide it in a ditch."

"We're back to him standing in the road with the goddam box."

"Maybe someone came along and he hitched a ride."

Laredo nodded glumly. "Let's wait for the stage driver."

The driver returned to the station late the next afternoon. He remembered the man who got off the stage at the edge of town with a box. "It was wrapped in an old blanket. Sewed into it, I think."

He rode with them to the outskirts and pointed out the place. "It was right here—give or take a dozen feet. I let 'im out and he pulled the thing out of the boot and we went on."

"Was there a cart or a wagon waiting for him?"

The driver shook his head. "No. Nothing."

Laredo looked beyond the road. In the field were a number of shacks, and as he looked an old man came out of one and sat down by a small fire.

Glancing at Pete, Laredo stepped across the ditch and walked over the weedy field to the shacks. Pete shrugged and followed.

The old man saw them coming and waved. He was dirty and unshaven, wearing rags. There was a blackened coffee pot on a crude grill, the water beginning to boil.

"Howdy, gents. . . ."

"Howdy," Laredo said. "How're you this afternoon?"

"Tolerable." The old man looked at them curiously. "You goin' to run us offen here?"

"No. Not at all."

The old man looked relieved. "Got some coffee b'ilin' in a minute. You care f'any?"

"No thanks," Laredo said. He looked at Pete and saw the other was smiling.

The old man, his total belongings worth possibly a half dollar, was sitting on an old blue blanket, wrapped around the steel shipment box.

About the Author

ARTHUR MOORE is the author of thirteen westerns including THE KID FROM RINCON and TRAIL OF THE GATLINGS, published by Fawcett Books. He lives in Westlake Village, California, where he is at work on a new Bluestar Western.